WORLD'S END

CULLEN & BAIN 2

ED JAMES

OTHER BOOKS BY ED JAMES

SCOTT CULLEN MYSTERIES SERIES

1. GHOST IN THE MACHINE
2. DEVIL IN THE DETAIL
3. FIRE IN THE BLOOD
4. STAB IN THE DARK
5. COPS & ROBBERS
6. LIARS & THIEVES
7. COWBOYS & INDIANS
8. HEROES & VILLAINS

CULLEN & BAIN SERIES

1. CITY OF THE DEAD
2. WORLD'S END (June 2020)
3. HELL'S KITCHEN (August 2020)

CRAIG HUNTER SERIES

1. MISSING
2. HUNTED
3. THE BLACK ISLE

DS VICKY DODDS

1. TOOTH & CLAW
2. FLESH & BLOOD (August 2020)

DI SIMON FENCHURCH SERIES

PROLOGUE

Adam stood in the freezing darkness, shivering as he stuck his key in the lock and twisted. But it didn't open. 'Bloody head office. Too cheap to pay for a proper system.' Every day, Adam saw how cheap they were, but hey, a job's a job. He tried the key again and the door opened this time, with no rhyme or reason. He took a deep breath and stepped inside the supermarket.

The lights flickered on, lifting the gloom on the breezeblock walls. But not by much. The store's backroom was a giant cube filled with empty metal cages. The deep freeze was just to the side, humming away, so he walked over to the door through to the front.

And it was absolutely boiling, like the heater had been working ten to the dozen all night. He just knew he was going to lose a couple of hours trying to get the standard-rate boiler repair guy down to Edinburgh from all the way up in Crieff. Yet more cheapness from head office.

And a stale smell hung on the air, like someone had left a packet of steak mince out all night. Or a whole cage of it. If there was one thing Adam knew, it was people leaving meat out all night. Bane of his effing life. He could picture fifty packets of mince browning and going all slimy.

'Hold the door!' Keith Ross was rushing down the street, his boots clumping off the frosty pavement, but he was a good three stone too heavy to keep that pace up for long. Not with *his* knees. He stopped, hard breath puffing in the freezing air, his distended belly hanging out of his "NO CHEMTRAILS" hoodie. In this weather, he still didn't wear a coat. Adam got a waft of dope, a tell-tale sign of yet another night on the hash bowls. At least he was wearing his official Ashworth's jacket, though the orange wasn't as bright as it should be. 'Cheers, boss. Couldn't find my key this morning.'

Adam locked the door behind him with a sigh. 'Keith, you live in Clermiston, we're in Gilmerton. That's two buses, especially at this hour. Meaning that if I insisted you went back home to collect that key, which is effing company property then I'll lose my cleaner for an hour. The hour which is the only time during the day you can do any real cleaning.'

'You seriously want me to go home?'

'No, I of course I don't. Just stop forgetting it.'

'No big deal, though, man.' Keith smiled at him. 'You're always here, bud. Or there's Have A Phil doing the bread.'

'You shouldn't call him that.' Adam waited for a nod. 'And what if Phil forgets his key and I've got the dentist?'

'The dentist at half six in the morning?' Keith's face twisted up. Cynical bastard was always trying to pick holes in stuff. But then his face brightened with some new mystery. 'You know if I quit, you'll never find anyone as cheap as me.'

Adam didn't doubt it, but then you pay peanuts, you get monkeys. 'And you'll struggle to find another job.' He gestured through the roasting backroom towards the cleaning store. 'Just get on with it, okay?'

No sign of Keith doing that. The big lump just stood there,

the overhead lights lost in his thick beard. 'You check those links I sent you?'

Adam vaguely remembered some messages on his phone that morning, but he was too bleary-eyed to focus on them. The pot of coffee had cleared the worst of his hangover, but it was already shaping up to be a day where he needed to schedule a nice snooze on the toilet. 'I was busy last night, sorry.'

'Busy nudging turps, aye?' Keith stepped forward, his glassy eyes glowing in the dark store. 'Found this cracking video about coronavirus. Apparently the CIA developed it, unleashed it on some bats in China. From space.'

'How did bats get into space?'

'Don't be daft.' Keith rolled his eyes. 'They targeted the bats from an orbital platform.'

'With lasers?'

'No.' But he didn't have an answer.

Time for Adam to twist the knife. 'If the CIA did it, how does that explain it infecting people in America?'

'Collateral damage.' Keith's shrug showed that's all the consideration that gaping hole needed. 'Plus, the kind of people most at risk of catching it are the ones who can't afford to get a test and can't afford to take two weeks off work in quarantine. Thinning out the herd.'

Always an answer for everything. What Adam wouldn't give to go back in time to before YouTube and all those nut-job conspiracy theories, and before pretty much everything else. 'All so the New World Order can institute a global government, aye?'

'Sure you didn't watch it?'

'Positive.' Adam patted his arm. 'I'll just check on the young lad, see how he's getting on.' He pointed to the cleaner's store cupboard again. 'Get on with it.'

'Aye, aye. It's *boiling* in here. I'm sweating like a bastard already.'

'So turn the heating down.'

'Aye, aye.' Keith shuffled off, stuffing in his earbuds to listen to yet another conspiracy freak podcast, or an audiobook about chemtrails turning frogs gay, or whatever new nonsense he was filling his head with.

Adam walked off in the opposite direction, passing through the rubber flaps into the store itself. He hit the first aisles and triggered the banks of lights to flash on.

It was set in pitch darkness—not a good sign—so he set off, the lights flashing on as he passed. He tried not to inspect each and every aisle for how badly they needed refilling. Tuesday night wasn't nightfill, so his team of underpaid idiots would stack up during the day. The way things used to be, but it meant they'd be chasing their tails all day until the store shut and the nightfill took over.

No toilet rolls, even with their rationing at the tills. Pretty soon people would start paying for things by the sheet. Or they'd move on to pasta or tins of tomatoes.

At the far end, the bread aisle was a complete disaster. The shelves were virtually empty, just the huddled remnant of yesterday's stock that hadn't been sold off to the yellow-item vultures in the final hour of trading last night. And no sign anyone had been in this morning. Young Phil should've been here at the crack of sparrow fart to take the bread delivery and start stocking up. Should've just about been finished by now too.

He checked his phone for messages from Phil, maybe saying he was self-quarantining, but there was just the YouTube link from Keith.

Either way, looked like he was going to have to do the whole lot himself.

And it was so effing hot. Still, the sooner he started, the sooner he'd get that bacon roll and that blissful sleep on the toilet. He stomped off, the shop now all bright and glaring, then through the doors to the back storeroom.

The storeroom was piled high with boxes ready for the compactor. No sign of Young Phil.

A loud squeak came from somewhere behind him. Made him jerk around.

But it was just Keith twisting that tap he was constantly moaning about, the one Adam would have to call another Crieff-based plumber to fix.

Adam cut through the narrow corridor between the boxes, just about wide enough to wheel a cage through and opened the main door. And there they were, the bread cages, unattended and freezing in the icy blast.

Six of white, two of wholemeal, another three of rolls and wraps and all that malarkey. Two of cakes.

And still no sign of Young Phil.

Effing useless.

Adam took the first cake cage and wheeled it inside. He stopped dead.

In an alcove between some empty cages, someone had scrawled a message over the scuffed floor tiles. "Love and kisses, the Evil Scotsman".

What the effing hell?

Next to it, a body lay in an Ashworth's uniform, covered from head to toe in yellow price-reduction stickers.

Young Phil.

Was he just messing about?

Adam charged over and went to shake him. But he stopped. There was something about not waking someone who was sleepwalking, wasn't there? And... Christ. Phil wasn't breathing.

He touched Phil's cheek. Ice cold. Dead.

And Adam would have to do the effing bread on his own.

1

BAIN

Sundance sits there in the meeting room, reams of paperwork in front of him. Place stinks of those pens and stale milk. DI Scott fuckin' Cullen. Pretty bastard, with that dimple in his cheek. Fancy new haircut, probably ordered by his new bird. Fresh clean look now he was a DI. *Acting* DI.

Can't believe this prick's my boss now. How times have changed.

He slides a copy of my annual appraisal over the table. Way bigger than usual, like *War and fuckin' Peace* compared to the usual pamphlet. And he's grinning away like a fuckin' clown. I've seen him do this before when he's shitting it about something. Sneaky wee toerag. He clears his throat into his fist, then stares into his hand like there's something there. Probably just bad news for yours truly.

'Since that case in Glasgow last month, I've been impressed by your application. You've turned a corner and are really gelling with the team. Thanks, Brian.'

Don't know what the arsehole expects of us, but I give him a shrug. 'Cheers.'

'There is one thing, though.' And there it is again, that fuckin' grin. Makes my blood boil, I tell you. 'I've received some concerning reports about some questionable remarks you've made to witnesses and members of the public.'

Aye, that'll be fuckin' chocolate. Doesn't take a genius like me to figure out who's been grassing. This prick has saddled me with two DCs. I know it's not Elvis, obviously, meaning it's Sundance's bum chum. Not exactly the kind of deductive reasoning I'm renowned for but, hey ho. 'DC Hunter should keep his thoughts to himself.'

'I didn't say it was him.'

'No?' Catch myself rubbing my nose. That big plook isn't going anywhere and it's hurting like a bastard. 'Might as well have hired a plane to write it across the fuckin' sky.'

'It wasn't him.'

That throws us. So who the fuck was it? Murray? That Polish bird? Fuckin' Budgie? Wait, I know who it fuckin' is. 'Was it Chantal?'

'Brian, can you stop focusing on who passed on their concerns to me, and start thinking about how you might want to change your behaviour? Okay?'

Pretty fuckin' far from okay, but in this place, you've got to play the game. Even if you don't like the fuckin' rules. And they stink like fresh dog shit, especially since they fucked it royally and changed it all to Police Scotland. 'Fine.'

Prick looks like he's expecting more. Eyes wide, like he's in one of them Japanese cartoons.

Walls are closing in on us, I swear. 'Do you know what I'm alleged to have said?'

'It's largely to do with your swearing. Now I let a lot of things slide, but you need to tone down your use of the F-word.'

Fuck it, for fuckin' fuck's sake. My fists are clenched and I'm ready to take this fucker on. 'This is fuckin' bullshit, Sundance. Crystal fuckin' Methven is always with the sodding this, sodding that and—'

'That's another thing.' Sundance rifles through his papers. Bringing a ream of five hundred sheets into a suspect interview is the oldest trick in the book. Try to make them think you've got a shit ton of stuff on them. Well, I started it and I don't appreciate this wee nyaff trying it on with me. He pulls out a page halfway through and... Shite, it actually looks like the pages might have something printed on them, after all. Shite, shite, shite. 'You've got to stop giving everyone nicknames.'

Cheeky bastard. 'You're just as bad.'

'How?'

'You started Crystal Methven.'

'That wasn't me.'

'You were going through a *Breaking Bad* boxed set at the time, if I recall.'

Prick's blushing now. He's rubbing up against the fuckin' ropes and the champion here's winding up a sucker punch. Nobody's taking my fuckin' belts off me!

And then I realise—it was his ex who came up with the nickname, wasn't it? Sitting there in their grubby wee flat just off the Royal Mile, watching Walter White and Jesse Pinkman cooking up crystal meth. Crystal Methven. Bet their sides were fair splitting. Ho ho ho. And he fuckin' hates her, doesn't he? Another wee screw to twist and turn.

'Brian, I need you to focus on the message here. You can't use nicknames to people's faces.'

'I take it all back. I'm sorry.' That gets a smile from the smug wanker. 'But behind their backs is okay? Come on, that's snide as fuck.'

'As a way of letting off steam, it's fine. I don't mind people calling me names behind my back.'

'You seem to hate Sundance.'

'To my face.' The arsehole jabs a finger at us, almost touching my beak. 'And you know why.'

I don't give him any satisfaction or any more ammo. But he's not getting away with this. Not after last time. I'll take the prick down, but first... 'You should be very careful. I've got friends in high places.'

The prick sits back in his chair with a little squeak. Maybe he farted. Out of fear, I hope. The ref's counting down from ten, and Sundance is clean out of it. He reaches over the table for my paperwork and writes a 3 in the box.

'A three? That's it?'

'You think you deserve a four?'

'Sundance, I *know* I deserve a five. I've been in that seat, worn those shoes. I know what's a three and a four and a fuckin' five.'

Prick looks like he wants to give us a 2 and stick us on an action contract. Move us out of the door. But my warning has spooked him and he's reeling. Knows who I'm talking about, too. That "Acting" bit of his title suddenly seems mighty tenuous.

'Look, if you keep up the discipline you've shown since Glasgow, if you cut down the swearing, the nicknames and the bullying, then *maybe* we'll consider you for a four at your full-year appraisal.'

'This is a shit sandwich, Scott. Two bits of vague good news wrapped around a really smelly turd.'

Getting no reaction from him now. Maybe the ref didn't count him out.

'I used to do these appraisals on you back in the day. Used to have to warn you about your drinking and shagging around.'

'That was a long time ago.'

'Aye? I know what you were up to at Tulliallan with that wee minx from Livingston.'

Oh, I've fuckin' done it now. Face twisted up and sneering and his mouth's hanging open. He's *raging*.

But his moby goes. He reaches into his jacket pocket for it and checks it, then says 'Cunt' under his breath. Way stronger language than what I've been warned about. Two-faced arse-candle. 'Sorry, thought this was on mute.' He kills it and puts it away. 'Now, where were we? Oh, aye.' He sighs at us. Big habit with the boy, always at it. Whether he's bored or stressed or what, who knows, but you can tell if he's in the trap next to you in the gents just by the timbre of the sigh. 'Brian. This is precisely what I'm talking about. You keep lashing out at the people trying to help you. Like me. You need to stop reacting and to start listening, okay?'

'Right.'

'Don't "right" me.' His phone goes again. 'For crying out loud.' He stabs the screen. 'Brian, you're a detective sergeant and I need you to focus. This isn't working in a call centre, though you're welcome to try that.' Cheeky bastard thinks he's funny. 'I need you to be on your A-game. Our job is to solve serious crimes, not score points against each other.'

'Be very careful what you're saying to me, Scott.'

Another big sigh from the boy.

Before he can launch myself at me, the door opens and bugger me, if it's not Angela Caldwell. Suited and booted too. When did she come back? And Christ, I forget how tall she is. Six four at least.

Shite, I know exactly what he's up to here. Bringing back his old sidekick, Batgirl, and training her up as a DS to replace yours truly. Fuck that shit.

Sundance gets up and walks over to the door. 'Sorry, Angela, I'm busy with—'

I can't hear the rest, but she's whispering in his ear. Wanker.

'Gilmerton? Okay.' Sundance beckons for us to get to my feet. 'Get your coat, Sergeant, we'll finish this later.'

2

―――――

CULLEN

A queue of cars lined the side street in Gilmerton, impatient shoppers desperate to get inside for their morning bargains, all just sitting there. Miles away from the city centre, and it didn't have that Edinburgh feeling. More like a small town that had been swallowed up.

Cullen wound down his window and let the blast of honking horns into the car. He just knew it was going to take hours getting round it.

His phone rang. Methven.

He answered it with a sigh. 'Sir, traffic's bad, but I'm just about there.'

'Excellent. I'm unable to attend, so you're my eyes and ears, okay?'

Cullen inched the car forward. 'What's stopping you coming here?'

'I've got meetings all day. Unavoidable ones. I'm lending my expertise to a case DCS Soutar is running up in Dundee. Please take a lead there today, okay?'

'Okay.'

'How did DS Bain take it?'

'I didn't get round to delivering the real message, sir.'

'I see.'

'I've deferred his appraisal until we've dealt with this case.'

'Well. It's important that we serve notice as soon as possible, don't you think?'

'I do, but… It's not easy, sir.'

'The price of being a DI, Scott. You've wanted this for a long time, so you need to show me you can handle the pressure.'

'Sir.'

And Methven was gone.

Just fantastic.

And this traffic wasn't clearing. Nothing coming this way, though.

Cullen flicked on his lights and checked his mirrors, then gave a blast of siren and pulled out into the oncoming lane. A bus's brakes squealed, but there was enough of a gap for him to squeeze into the small car park. He had to stop just inside.

A pimply young uniform guarded the entrance, shivering in the cold morning. He didn't take much of a look at Cullen's proffered warrant card before letting him through.

The supermarket car park was mercifully empty, save for the grimy SOCO van. Cullen parked next to Jimmy Deeley's silver Mercedes. The pathologist was here too. Some good news for once.

The pool Mondeo's engine rumbled to a halt and Cullen got out into a teeming downpour that seemed to come from nowhere. Pelting down in stair rods, as his gran would've said. He jogged off across the battered tarmac.

The store was medium-sized, the steep roof tapering to a point above the orange Ashworth's logo, bright against the dark clouds, the cheesy "We're Well Worth It!" slogan dimmer in comparison.

Through the glass, the café was filled with his squad. Bain was tucking into a bacon roll, tomato sauce smearing his lips. And no doubt Cullen would pay for that. Or at least it'd come out of Methven's budget.

No sign of Caldwell, so Cullen entered the supermarket, soaking already.

A big paw stopped his progress. 'Scott?'

DC Craig Hunter stood there, chewing. He towered over Cullen. Not many would try to get past the big bastard. His shaved head and hard jawline would warn most off at a good distance.

'Alright, Craig. Tell me Bain's not helping himself through there?'

'Wish I could.' Hunter passed him over a clipboard and took another bite of his egg roll. 'He's put me on managing the crime scene.'

Cullen scrawled his name and handed it back. 'I know I can be a twat at times, but is he taking the piss?'

'Relax, mate. The store manager's cooking up stock that would go off today. Anderson's shut the place for the day so he can get a clear run at the forensics.'

Cullen looked around for James Anderson and any of his cabal, but no sign. He clocked a big guy looking over at them. 'Who's that?'

'That's the manager.'

Cullen wanted to avoid him. All he'd get is complaints about not being able to open. 'Where's the body?'

Hunter tossed him a crime scene suit. 'Through the back.'

EITHER THE SUITS were getting smaller or Cullen was getting

bigger. Felt like he needed to go up at least one size. He didn't want to consider that he was becoming a fat bastard, or that it was Hunter's way of motivating him to join him in another park-based bootcamp session, the kind that was hard to walk away from. Or for days afterwards.

Someone barred the entrance, though his full-body smurf suit seemed to fit him better. Lamb-chop sideburns visible through the mask. Paul "Elvis" Gordon. He knew to fill out the form on Cullen's behalf, though. 'See when I told you at my appraisal that I didn't want to just do CCTV and all that shite, this isn't what I had in mind.'

'I appreciate you taking one for the team, Paul.' Cullen patted his arm as he glided past.

No matter how much effort supermarkets made to induce that warm fuzzy feeling to the customers out front, through the back it was like a Soviet gulag in deepest Siberia. But it was so hot in here, they'd need to stick everything in the deep freeze just to keep it cool. The store's back room was all bare concrete blocks, the poured floor filled with empty cages. Pretty much identical to the Ashworth's Cullen had worked in back home in Dalhousie when he was still at school. Probably built them all to a single template in the mid-Eighties expansion.

Cullen snuck between the empty cages and headed towards the arc lights, probably wasting all that electricity on just illuminating more cages rammed with bread and cakes. Five other suited figures worked away, one photographing, one cataloguing and the rest dusting away.

A man lay on the concrete, wearing the store's orange and black uniform. A pricing gun lay by his feet and he was covered in yellow reduced-price stickers, just his face exposed. He looked maybe nineteen or twenty. And a message was scrawled next to him on the floor in black marker pen. Cullen squinted at it. "Love and Kisses, the Evil Scotsman". Weird and weirder.

Cullen couldn't tell what had killed him, but suffocation was what he'd be getting odds on.

Two more male figures stood over the body, one holding a medical bag, his cheeks rounded like he was smiling. 'Ah, young Skywalker.'

'Professor Deeley.'

The other man shook his head, the precisely engineered goatee visible through the mask identifying him as James Anderson. 'Acting DI Skywalker, more like.' Anderson's nasal rasp. 'Jimmy, you mind if I pull these stickers off?'

'So long as you've photographed it, I couldn't give a hoot. The Acting DI here is the arbiter of our work.'

'Go for it, James.'

'Excellent.' Anderson seemed to take great relish in squatting down and easing the stickers free. Not the clean strike of a doctor removing something, more picking away at a scab on your knee.

Deeley stepped round the number tags to join Cullen. 'Well, Scott, it's been a while.'

'Hasn't it.' Cullen kept his gaze on Anderson's work. 'Thought you were retiring?'

'Staying on for another couple of years. Got a nice pay bump after all that austerity. I went through hell, I tell you. Hell.'

'You have to buy your new Mercedes every other year?'

'You try having four kids, three at university, and the other one discovering himself in Tibet...'

That was the last thing Cullen ever wanted to do. 'So what have we got?'

'A deep mystery.' Deeley shook his head. 'I'll admit that I'm struggling here. No idea what caused his death. I mean, it could be anything. Despite his age, it could be a heart attack, and someone's decided to play a prank thinking he was just asleep. But... okay. There are no signs of blunt force or penetrating trauma, and he doesn't seem to be leaking anywhere. No obvious signs of acute drug usage, but toxicology will fill in those blanks.'

Cullen had seen worse, that was for sure. 'So we treat it like it's a murder until we know differently. Aye?'

'Well, I'll advise you now that the post-mortem is going to take a *long* time.'

'Why?'

'Backed up, and laughing boy Anderson here is even worse.'

Cullen gritted his teeth. 'Anything I can go on?'

'For once, I'm as clueless as your good friend Brian Bain.'

Cullen was thankful for the mask hiding his grin. 'He's not my friend.'

'Well, based on the lividity, the level of rigor and liver temperature...' Deeley clicked his tongue a few times. 'A very loose approximation as to the time of death, not accounting for the extra ambient heat, would be...' He tilted his head to the side, sucking in like he'd just bitten a lemon. 'Five o'clock this morning. But could be as early as two, maybe even midnight. I mean, it's boiling in here.'

Cullen checked the body again. The shirt was soaked with sweat, so that at least played in to the story.

Anderson eased off the final stickers from around the victim's mouth and stepped aside, revealing a cavalier-style moustache and soul patch pairing. 'Shug, can you get this?'

The photographer knelt in front of the body and took a few snaps.

Anderson finished placing the stickers inside a bag, then passed them to a clipboard-wielding female CSI. 'Bag and tag, Mel.' He cracked his knuckles, the blue nitrile softening the crunch, and looked up at Cullen and Deeley. 'I'm thinking you don't cover someone's mouth unless you've shoved something inside, right?'

Cullen shrugged. 'That or you've killed them because of something they've said.'

'Let's just see.' Anderson leaned towards the body. 'Now, if I just say "open sesame"...' He prised the stiff lips apart, then jerked back. 'Ah, Christ.'

Cullen shifted position to get a better view. Still couldn't see anything. 'What is it?'

'That's *rank*.' Amid a barrage of camera flash, Anderson reached out his fingers and pulled out a strip of glistening meat, red and raw, but slightly browned at the edges. '*Beef*.'

Deeley was grinning. 'And what's the matter?'

'I'm vegan.' Anderson grabbed another bag. 'This is minging.'

Deeley winked at him. 'You know how you tell if someone's vegan?'

Anderson frowned. 'No?'

'They tell you.'

A wall of laughter burst out from the team of SOCOs.

'Fuck sake.' Anderson stuffed the slice of meat inside the bag, then reached into the victim's mouth again. 'Christ, there's at least half a pound in here.'

Deeley nodded, all professional now. 'I'll have a root around in his digestive system for any more, once I get round to it.'

Cullen had no idea what any of this meant.

'This place...' Elvis was standing next to him, arms folded. No sign of where he'd dumped his clipboard. Maybe he'd found a uniform to take on the task. 'My mate's ex lived round the corner from here. This place was the source of a meat poisoning scandal a few years ago. Someone was sticking strychnine in the mince.'

Cullen turned to Deeley. 'Think it's possible he was poisoned?'

'I mean, it's possible.' Deeley clicked his tongue a few times. 'Or he was suffocated. Again, we need to run tests and, again, it's going to take a long time.' Deeley winked at Cullen. 'And I think we know differently now. This is clearly a murder.'

'I'M THE DAY SHIFT MANAGER.' Adam Searle's head was a good few sizes too big for his body and shaved smooth. Dark stubble from the tips of his ears, streaked with silver, and dark rings around his eyes. His Ashworth's polo shirt was buttoned up to his chin, but spidery hair still crawled out. 'I found the body. Horrible business.'

The café was empty now, but still had that smell of fried bacon, a sharp tang that wouldn't shift. Bain wasn't around, but then that wasn't a surprise. He seemed to have a radar for Cullen's presence.

Cullen sipped coffee—not bad if a bit weak—while taking the measure of the store manager, seeing how he reacted to silence.

Searle just sat there, staring into space. Finding a body would do that to you. A colleague would be even worse, unless his name was Brian Bain.

But Angela Caldwell had other plans. 'And you know him, right?'

Searle focused on her. 'His name's Philip Turnbull.'

Caldwell raised her eyebrows, her lips an O. But Cullen was one step ahead of her. Detective Superintendent Jim Turnbull, their boss's boss. He'd need to check any relation. Or rather, Methven would.

'Some guys here call him "Have a Phil".'

'Oh? Why?'

'They were calling him "Phil McCracken", so he started that name himself to shut them up.'

She folded her arms. 'It's not because he was trying it on with female members of staff?'

'Nah, think he's gay.'

'Did he ever try it on with any male colleagues?'

'No.' Searle shut his eyes. 'I shouldn't talk about him like this.'

'It's perfectly natural.' She gave him a smile, but still kept her arms tight around her. 'It's how people cope.'

'Right.'

'Did he work here full-time?'

'Part-time. He's a student at Edinburgh uni. Second year, I think. In at five, on his own. Stocks up the bread, then he's off by nine to his lectures. Good kid. Hard worker.'

'But the bread was inside the store first thing?'

'Aye.'

'Okay.' Cullen was a step ahead of Deeley now. It either meant the victim had brought the bread in, or the killer had. Or Searle had. Bloody hell, it was a nest of vipers. 'And you don't have CCTV of it?'

'That's right. Sorry.'

Convenient. 'Do you know who was in here last night?'

'Nobody. Tuesday's not nightfill.' Searle sniffed. 'It's only five nights a week. Tuesday and Sunday off. My guys would've had to stock up during the day shift. Just topping it up before Brendan's guys come in at night. That's Brendan Webster, the nightfill manager.'

'Does Mr Turnbull work for him?'

'No, he's under my wing.'

'The yellow price-reduction stickers, that seems—'

'Vultures.'

'Excuse me?'

'It's what we call them, the men who hang around waiting for us to put the yellow stickers on the stuff. And it's always men. Some hunter-gatherer psychology, wanting to bring home the best dinner or something. Can imagine it worked well on the plains of Africa, but when you're serving up out-of-date mince?' He shut his eyes and swallowed hard.

'You okay?'

'Just processing it.'

Cullen gave him a few more seconds. The door opened and Bain popped his head through, then cleared off before Cullen could signal him. 'Think any of these "vultures" could have a beef against Mr Turnbull?' He regretted using that word. Gripe, maybe, not beef.

Searle thought it through. 'Hard to say. I mean, surely nobody would kill someone over not reducing a load of bread to 10p, would they?'

'I've seen weirder stuff.'

'Really?'

'Really.' Cullen smoothed down the page on his notebook. 'Notice anything strange when you found the body?'

'Like what? He was covered in yellow stickers.' Searle's forehead twitched. 'Wait. Was there something inside his mouth?'

And there it was. Hold back the evidence and watch them implicate themselves by knowing more than they should.

'What was in there?'

Cullen gave a slight shrug.

'Meat?'

So many good guesses here.

'Was it meat?'

'What makes you think that?'

He scratched at the stubble on his head. 'There was a meat-poisoning scandal here a couple of years back. Had to shut the store for a fortnight. Closed the butcher counters for all twenty-five stores in Scotland. Replaced it all with pre-packed meat.'

And there was a second suspect already. 'You know if the old butcher is still around?'

Searle locked eyes with Cullen. 'You're looking at him.'

And back to one suspect.

'They gave me this job when they shut the counter. Not all the lads were as lucky. Some got laid off. But I stayed on. Sometimes wonder if they were the lucky ones.' He locked eyes with Cullen. 'What meat was it?'

'We don't know yet.'

'But chicken and pork look different from beef, right?'

Cullen nodded. 'I'd say it was beef, but it could be lamb or venison.'

'And it was stuffed in there?'

Cullen nodded, then left a long pause. 'Know anything about it?'

'What, you think I did it?'

'Did you?'

'Mate. I found the kid. Of course I didn't kill him.'

'Didn't say you did.'

Searle's mouth hung open.

'You seem to know a hell of a lot for someone who just happened to find the body.'

'I'm trying to be helpful here.'

'It wouldn't the first time someone had pulled that trick. Pretending to find a body. I need to know your movements last night, sir. Right through until you found the body.'

'Well, I clocked off here at the back of six. Bus home, then I watched the football.'

'What was the score?'

'Can't mind.'

More alarm bells ringing now. 'Who was playing?'

'Liverpool. Against Atlético de Madrid.' Pronounced as if he'd grown up in the city.

'And you can't remember the score?'

'I... fell asleep.'

Cullen could smell it now, the telltale reek of second-hand booze, that thick musty scent, partly hidden by sweat and own-brand deodorant. 'What time?'

'No idea. Before half-time, I think. It was boring, to be honest. One of those ones they'd say was like a chess match. My old man was a huge Liverpool fan. Took me down a few times.'

'And this morning?'

'I told you. Turned up here, place was melting. I let the cleaner in, then found Phil. Dead.' Searle shut his eyes and clenched his jaw, sobbing gently. If he was the killer and this was all an act, well, he was due an Oscar.

Cullen was in two minds about what to do here.

Treat him as suspect number one. He didn't have too much, just a couple of assumptions married together to give some doubt. The meat was a clear signifier of guilt, that's for sure.

But was he really the killer?

He needed to check it all out. 'You said there's no CCTV in here?'

'That's right.'

'What about outside?'

THE SECURITY ROOM was next to the manager's office, a window-less box that smelled of mushrooms and muddy tea. It was filled with large TV screens and recording equipment. No sign of a security guard, though.

'I was expecting your security officer in here?' Cullen was standing in the doorway, partly with a view to blocking Searle's exit, but mainly because there were two chairs and he'd let Angela sit in one.

Searle was in the main chair, working the jog wheel and winding the footage back through hours of darkness in infrared. 'Bob wasn't due in till ten.'

Cullen checked his watch. Ten past. 'So why isn't he here?'

'Told him not to come in.'

Cullen tried not to punch anything. 'You need to run that past me and my team, okay?'

'Oh, right.' Searle tapped the screen. 'There you go.'

The top-left quadrant of the display showed a young man unlocking the supermarket's back door and entering. As the door swung shut, he tapped a code into an alarm, an act visible on the top-right screen. The code was 4:56.

'That his usual arrival time?'

'Right. He does a stocktake, clears the shelves of out-of-code produce then—'

Angela was frowning. 'Out of code?'

'Out of date.'

'Right. After he's binned that, he waits until the bread delivery.' Searle played with the jog wheel, showing nothing in particular for fifteen minutes until Phil Turnbull wheeled a trolley through and started tossing loaves of bread. 'See, that's it there.'

The bottom left quadrant was blank, while the right showed a wide delivery door from outside, hidden in shadowy darkness.

'What's up with that camera?'

'Broken.'

'When?'

'About a month ago.' Searle winced. 'I have no end of hassle getting stuff fixed here. Head office up in Crieff insist on getting local firms to repair everything, no matter where the store is. If I want to change a lightbulb, some boy from Crieff needs to come down. That's like a two-hour drive or something, with traffic. And we've got stores in Dumfries and up in the Highlands.'

Cullen tried to pin it down to Searle, but sometimes it was just incompetence. 'Is this on tape?'

'Nope. It's cloud-based. Server in, you guessed it, Crieff. We normally don't have immediate access to it, but we've... We've had some issues with theft. We're losing more out the back door than on the front-end, if you catch my drift. So we've got checks at the end of the shift and I've got to review this footage. Constantly.'

Cullen had seen that before and was glad he didn't have to chase up some Crieff-based corporate suit to get access. 'Any signs of forced entry into the store this morning?'

'All looked fine.'

'Were the doors locked when you arrived?'

'Sure.'

On the other screen, a lorry pulled up with "West & Hall Baker's" signage. Hazards on, mid-grey on the monitor. The driver hopped out and rang a bell. The other two displays showed Philip Turnbull's movements as he walked over to the door.

As the door slid up and over, Cullen braced himself for the delivery driver clonking Phil Turnbull on the head with a length of lead pipe. But he just helped him get the bread inside the store. Five minutes to unload, then he was gone, leaving Philip to shut the door behind him.

Angela was frowning, though. 'Play that again. The last cages.'

'Okay.' Searle jockeyed it back to them taking the last pair inside.

'Stop.' Angela leaned forward to point at the screen.

Just as they wheeled the cages in, a shadowy figure sneaked past them into the store.

3
———

Bain

Tell you what this game is all about, when you get down to it.

Control.

Don't let anybody tell you otherwise. None of those twats taking courses at fuckin' Tulliallan, or any of the fuds in charge of anything. It's all about control.

While Sundance is prancing around downstairs in the public café—obviously closed to the public and cleared out of all perishable products by yours truly—I'm up here in the staff canteen, frying up some fuckin' lovely looking Spanish omelettes, even if I do say so myself. Someone's left a chopped peppers mix and some chorizo in the fridge along with some organic free-range eggs. Well, I'm not letting that go to waste.

And the boys are appreciating it. All three of the lads I've taken under my wing. Elvis, Hunter and Buxton, that big cockney wide-boy, acting like he's selling marrows or whatever down some market in the fuckin' East End. Though now I mention it, I think he's from out west somewhere. Might be a QPR fan.

And I'm in control. My boys are taking up three of the big round tables, each one interviewing a member of staff, the gorgeous smells must be making them hungry as fuck. Somebody's stomach's rumbling, mind.

Not that many have pitched up, thanks to that fanjo Sundance is grilling downstairs. Searle, the boss, sending them all home.

Speaking of grilling, I take the three omelettes out from under there and slide them on the plates. Sprinkle some of that grated gruyere on top—not my first choice—and fold them over. They look first-class. And the gas burner up here is the fuckin' bambers. Need to get one at home, but my significant other doesn't like gas, not that I get a fuckin' say and I do all the cooking. All about electricity. Induction or whatever it's called, and you can't get the same control as one of these bad boys.

Control, see?

Anyway, mine is ready now and nobody will mind if I stick a ton more cheese on than the other ones. My mouth's watering as I slice into the bubbly egg with a fork, then I'm drooling as I eat it. And it's fuckin' delicious. The sausage is all caramelised round the edges and the peppers are tangy.

Man, I do need to get a burner. Control.

That prick Hunter's looking over at us, like he thinks I'd conceive of not making an omelette for one of my boys. Well, dream on, big guy. He might be a total fanny, but he's getting some of Uncle Bri's eggy goodness. I give him the nod and he goes back to listening to the cleaner.

Big guy, got that metal warrior look, like he's burst his eardrums hammering them with fuckin' Whitesnake or Bon Jovi or those newer ones bands with big stupid trousers. Korn or something. Or those arseholes with the gimp masks.

Hunter might be Sundance's new bum chum—poor Buxton used to have that dubious pleasure, but he must've mislaid the golden ticket somewhere.

Hunter's not a bad officer, have to say. And boy does he need a nickname. I know Sundance wants me to stop using them so publicly, and telling me to lose my morals and be a backstabbing cunt like him. Only thing I've seen him hunting is his own fuckin' tail, mind. What about Cunter? Too on the nose? 'But you were here when Mr Searle found the body?'

The big cleaner lad nods at him. His nostrils must be twitching at the heavenly scents coming his way. Bet he could snarf all four omelettes in one mouthful and still be back for more.

Fuck this. I leave my plate and half the omelette, and head over. I'd pull up the chair, scrape the legs over the floor to unnerve the big bastard, but it's all bolted in and locked down. All I can do is not go arse over tit as I sit between them. Give the boy a few seconds to look at us—when really it's that bacon from downstairs repeating on us and I have to cover a burp with my fist. 'I understand how hard it must've been to find that body.'

The boy frowns. 'I didn't find him. It was Mr Searle.'

'Right, but you were here?'

'Aye, aye. I'd left my key at home and we had a wee chat and...'

I wave at Elvis and he looks over. 'Can you get a hold of these keys?'

'Sure thing.' But he just sits there.

'Should only be three of us have them.' The cleaner boy's got a T-shirt reading "NO CHEMTRAILS". The words are in that *Ghostbusters* thing, the red circle and it's kind of scored out.

I point at it. 'Does that not cancel it out?'

He looks at the T-shirt, then frowns at us. 'Eh?'

'It's like you're saying no "no chemtrails", so you want chemtrails.'

Boy's puzzled by that. 'You know what they're doing with them?'

'I've heard a few things.'

'It's how the CIA puts mind-control drugs in the atmosphere. They just want us to be pliable, compliant subjects.'

'That right?'

'You don't believe me?'

'I like to keep an open mind.' Have to cover another burp. 'So, you talk to the young lad about chemtrails?'

'Phil, aye.' The big guy sniffs. Should really get his name, but he's talking freely now so I don't want to interrupt him. 'He's more into 9/11 truther stuff, and I dig that, don't get me wrong.' He looks right at us, crazy and swivel-eyed. 'You see that new Art Oscar video about coronavirus?' The way he says it, it's like he's seen the word written down a ton of times but never said it out loud. Even though he looks like the sort of weirdo who's on YouTube 24/7. 'He sent it to me. Big fan of Art Oscar.'

'Right. I've heard of the boy.' I glance over at Elvis. The number of times that idiot's sent me links to his patter on the *New Yorker*, I tell you. Still haven't clicked one.

'That's why I think he's been killed.' The big guy sits back, folding his tattooed arms across his manboobs. 'They don't want the truth to get out.'

I'm fiddling with my phone here, checking the boy on YouTube, and I find that video, so I look this idiot in the eye again. 'So I should be looking for another half a million corpses, aye?'

'Eh?'

I show him the screen, even let Hunter inspect it, though quite why he's still sitting here is anybody's guess as he's being next to useless. 'Half a million people have watched this. Means the message is already out there. Should we be warning Art Oscar?'

The boy's blushing. Whoever this clown is, he's not got a clue who did this to Young Phil.

'Thanks for your time, son.' I get to my feet and step away, but can't get my fuckin' foot over the fuckin' chair, so I go flying and sprawl all over the floor.

Dead silence, then all the other fannies are laughing at us. Especially Hunter. Fuckin' joker.

Only one move here. Laugh along with them. I jump up to my feet and walk off, raising my hand to soak up the applause like I've just scored the third goal of a perfect hat-trick at Ibrox in front of the Govan stand.

Elvis is over by the cooker, tucking into an omelette. 'Cracking laugh there, Bri.'

'Need an icebreaker in here, though it's fuckin' melting.' I grab my plate and start on the rest of my omelette. 'You getting anything?'

'Not much. Cullen had me looking at some security footage. Couldn't get much more from it than big Angie Caldwell could.'

'Figures. I'll keep you away from that pish, don't you worry.'

'Cheers, Bri. But I think we should speak to the cop who answered the call.'

'Eh?' I accidentally spit egg all over the boy. 'That was you, you tube!'

'Not here.' He shakes his head. 'Phil Turnbull's got a police record, Bri. My lad said he tried to assault a neighbour when he was pished.'

4

CULLEN

Searle was in his office talking on the phone, but so low he couldn't be heard. Didn't look like it was going the way he wanted, though.

Cullen waited out in the corridor, checking his mobile for messages. Nothing, which wasn't a good sign. He needed to pin down Bain and get an update from him. But he was nowhere to be seen and that was *definitely* never a good sign.

'Scott?' Angela was in the security room doorway, so Cullen inched closer to her. 'Well, Elvis wasn't much help.'

'Did he say what he's been up to?'

'No, but I could smell eggs cooking.' She hefted up a service laptop, that looked like it weighed more than she did. 'Still, he helped me get it on this.' She held it out.

Cullen took the machine from her and it was almost too heavy to hold in one hand. A photo roll of maybe fifteen stills, from a dark boot appearing on the right side, to the same boot disappearing into the store. The best shot was the tenth, but that was still blurry as hell. 'Anything he can do to make them sharper?'

'Nope. Well, this is having been processed.'

Bollocks.

'This is no use, is it? We can't pin it down to anyone.'

Angela didn't have anything other than a shrug. 'Afraid not.'

'Right.' Cullen took the laptop into Searle's office.

He'd finished his phone call and was looking out of the window.

'Sir, I—'

'Jesus!' Searle jumped like someone had plugged him into the mains.

'Sorry.' Cullen rested the laptop on the desk in front of him. 'One last time, do you recognise them?'

Searle gave it a good look, but pushed it away. 'Sorry.'

'Where were you at this time?'

Searle frowned. 'That clearly isn't me.'

He wasn't correct, though. The footage could've been anyone from the skinniest rake right up to the fattest bastard. 'Even so.'

'I was on the bus.'

'You got a Ridacard?'

'I do.' Searle reached into his pocket for a brown leather wallet. He flipped it open to a photo card of him with more hair.

Angela took it off him and snapped a photo. She handed it back and whispered to Cullen, 'I'll contact the bus company.' And she left them to it.

'You can't think I killed Phil?'

Cullen shrugged, but said nothing.

'Christ.' Searle gestured out of the window. Across the car park, two uniforms blocked the entrance, dealing with red-faced shoppers honking their horns. 'Listen, I'm under pressure from head office to open this place.'

'Not going to happen for a while. We've got to run forensics and process CCTV. You'll be lucky if it's open by the weekend.'

'Come on...'

'If your boss is giving you hassle, have them speak to mine.' Cullen handed over a business card. 'This is my boss's number. DCI Colin Methven.'

He sighed. 'Fine.'

'How did Mr Turnbull get along with your other members of staff?'

'Fine.'

'No gripes with anyone?'

'Nope.'

'Even the "Have a Phil" stuff?'

'Look, that's because someone tried to call him Phil McCracken.' Searle winced. 'Sometimes you need a decoy nickname, right?'

Cullen knew full well. 'Any run-ins with customers?'

'Not that I'm aware of.'

'Okay. Well, I need to speak to Mr Turnbull's next of kin. You know where I can find them?'

CULLEN PULLED into the parking space and got out. Gilmerton was still thriving and not seeing the sort of panic-buying happening elsewhere. Just a bunch of people going about their business as if the sky wasn't going to fall.

The Dark Horse pub was a grimy boozer that probably had sawdust on the floor to soak up all the spit. One of those places where it was at its busiest during the day, a huddle of men in their fifties and sixties supping pints of best and lager in front of the horse racing. Not that there was anywhere local to place the bets—the bookmakers a few doors along was shuttered, the owner dead a couple of years now and nobody picking up his business's poisoned chalice.

Except for the street drug dealing. Everyone wanted a piece of that pie.

Between the pub and the dead bookies was Turnbull's Craft Butchers, old-fashioned and traditional. Bright white interior showing a high level of cleanliness. A few industry posters in the window advertising how good meat was for growing kids. A handwritten sign advertising a freezer pack. The fridge ran round in a J-shape, with the strong reds of the mince, burgers and steaks nearest the window, next to the pinks of the pork and chicken, but walled off from the pies and the sausage rolls.

A ruddy face behind the counter, joyfully chatting to an elderly customer, then a final wave and the bell tinkled as the customer left him to it. He sat back against the till and cradled a cup of coffee, his wrist almost doubled back.

'Christ, Scott, it's like you want him to manfully take you over the counter.' DC Angela Caldwell swept past him and entered the butcher's.

Cullen almost regretted giving her her old job back. Then again, he needed some officers who could do their jobs, not just Bain and his clowns. He let out a sigh and followed her into the shop.

'And this is DI Cullen.' Angela smiled at the butcher. 'Do you have somewhere we can talk, Mr Turnbull?'

'Why?' The butcher's gaze swept between them, like a searchlight looking for hope in murky waters. 'What's happened?'

For a flat above a butcher's, Richard Turnbull's home was surprisingly large and well furnished. The bay window looked along a street Cullen couldn't remember the name of, but could vividly recall a drunken sexual encounter with a nurse in a flat halfway along.

Turnbull wasn't coping well. He was slumped on a mid-brown leather sofa, sobbing into his hands. He looked up with bleary eyes. 'You're *sure* it's him?'

'His manager discovered the body, sir. He confirmed it was your son.' Angela was sitting opposite him. Close, but not too close. Keeping up eye contact when he wanted it—and when he needed it—but giving him space and time to grieve, and to come to terms with the sudden extreme change to his life. Yeah, she was a pro.

Turnbull ran a hand over his face and stared up at the ceiling. 'I see.'

Angela sat back, giving him space again.

Cullen paced around the flat, peeking into the kitchen. Smelled of glue and paint, like it had just been done. And not by the kind of cowboys he could afford, but high-end people. Decent equipment too, brands he couldn't trace back to a language let alone pronounce or recognise.

Turnbull frowned at Angela. 'Was he murdered?'

'All we can say is that he was found dead at work in circumstances that seem suspicious. We are investigating and we will know more details once the pathologist has completed his examination.'

'But you will catch the animal who did this to my boy, won't you?'

'We'll try, sir.' She gave a warm smile. 'Anything you can give us about your son's life would certainly help with that.'

'You got kids?'

Angela nodded, but there was steel in her jaw. 'Two boys.'

Turnbull focused on Cullen. 'You?'

In most circumstances, Cullen would joke, 'Not that I know of,' and add in a cheeky wink. But not here, not now. 'No, sir.'

'Hell of a business this. Shouldn't have to bury your own son.'

'Is your wife around?'

'She's...' Turnbull shuffled forward on the sofa and clasped his hands together. 'My late wife inherited the business from her father. Sheena, her old man was a Richard too. Forbes, though. We renamed the place to our marital name.'

Angela creased her forehead. 'How's business been?'

'Booming, an exception on the high street these days.' Turnbull swallowed hard, then prodded his chest. 'Never thought I'd bury both of them. Sheena and Phil. And I'm the one with the triple bypass. Should be me that's on the slab, not my boy.' Moisture surrounded his eyes now. 'Christ, Phil. Why'd you have to leave me too?'

Angela sat back, flashing her eyebrows up for Cullen to take over.

He took the seat next to her and waited for eye contact with Turnbull. 'Can I ask why your son doesn't work downstairs?'

'He used to. After school and on Sundays. Used to get him out on the delivery bike.'

'But?'

Turnbull sighed. 'But we don't speak these days. Not since his mother passed on. Philip has been working at the supermarket most mornings, paying his way through university. He's studying business at Edinburgh. Smart kid but very pigheaded, just like his mother.'

'Do you mind me asking what happened between you?'

'I don't.' Turnbull hauled himself to his feet. He was short, barely up to Angela's head when she was still sitting. He walked over to the window and looked out along the street. 'Phil blamed me for her death. It was a stroke.' He shook his head. 'How could it be my fault?'

Cullen gave him more space and waited for him to turn

around to face them. 'Did your son ever talk about anyone, any enemies?'

Turnbull sat back on the sofa and picked up his cup. Must be freezing by now. He didn't drink it, just cradled it. 'Like I say, we didn't speak much. But I know one thing, his manager made his life hell.'

5

BAIN

Walking down the Royal Mile, I swear you smell so much ganja it's like being in student halls of residence back in the Nineties. Not that those pricks let me in.

Tell you, the softening of drugs policing has made this place a lot fuckin' worse. Like there, a pair of crusties openly smoking in the doorway of a shop. Dog on a string, dreadlocks, kaftans, skin-tight jeans. Pair of fannies. Proper grade-A skunk, too. Place is boarded up, mind, so it's not like they're preventing honest people getting in there. Used to sell woolly shite, never been in, but it's the principle of the thing, isn't it?

The boozer on the corner has had a facelift though. Time was, I'd head in there for a snifter. Never knew who was around, usually find a few people willing to pour their heart out to an officer of the law and DS Brian Bain made it his mission to lend that ear.

Can't believe I'm back there again, back at that rank. Fuck sake.

Anyhow, I head into World's End Close and it stinks of pish, like half the city's been using the place as a fuckin' toilet. Just off the Royal Mile, so fair enough. All those gays and their cottaging, getting the public toilets shut down. Nobody thinks about the real victims, do they? Men like me who can't go half an hour without a slash. And aye, nothing wrong with my prostate, thank you very much. Get the old thingy examined every three months whether it needs it or not.

Right, so the door's hanging open and I can't be arsed trying the buzzer, so I head on up. Knock on the door and wait. Five pockets until I find my phone. *Five.* Wish my subconscious would just stick it in the front right of my breeks, but no. Back right this time. One of those crusty arseholes could've just reached down and—

'Brian?' The door's open to a crack and she's peering out at us. Sharon, AKA DI Sharon McNeill of the East Division's Sexual Offences Unit. Though I tell you she should be investigated, not investigating. Her hair's really short nowadays at the sides, long fringe though. Used to call her Butch, mainly to wind up Sundance, but she's actually fuckin' tidy. Lost a ton of weight, hasn't she, and not where it counts. Oof ya.

I give her the old, infamous Bain grin, known to warm the hearts of a million women and a good few fellas I'm not too proud to admit. 'Hi, Sharon, you well?'

There's a fucking massive cat swarming round her feet. Big ginger bastard. Well, blonde maybe. But he's huge. And looks like a right cunt. I wave down at him. 'You've got a thing for gingers.'

'Excuse me?'

'Well, Cullen is a bit—'

'We split up.'

'Right, I know that but I was just—'

'Is there a reason you're here, Sergeant?'

Oooooh, get her. Time was, I was DI to her DS, but now it's all flip reversed and... 'You mind if I come in?'

'I do, as it happens.'

'Come on, Sharon, I need—'

'Brian, for a detective, you're not very attentive, are you?' She picks up the cat and holds him in her arms, but the big bastard is giving me the purest evils, I swear. 'It's a Tuesday morning and I'm at my flat when I should be at work.'

'Aye, aye. I spoke to your gaffer and he said you're on holiday. So here I am.'

'And the last person I want to see on my holiday is you.' She narrows her eyes. 'Well, Scott is the only one worse, but you're not much better.'

'Ever the charmer.' The smile isn't going to work on her, is it? 'Need to talk to you about a neighbour of yours, one Philip Richard Turnbull.'

A huff of a sigh, then she turns heel. 'You better come in, then.'

So I follow her inside and shut the door behind me. Place is fuckin' rammed with boxes. 'You moving house or something?'

She puts the cat down and cups a hand round her ear. 'Can you hear Sir Arthur Conan Doyle spinning in his grave?' She shakes her head at me. 'Talk of the master detective... Yes, Brian, I'm moving house.'

'Oh aye?'

'Bought a three-bedroom place in Ravencraig.'

'That's brave. Eat their fuckin' young there. How many cats can you fit in that place?'

'I'd offer you a cup of tea, but I'd just spit in it.'

'Sure it'd make it taste that little bit sweeter.'

As if she couldn't narrow her peepers any further, she does. 'What do you want to know about Philip Turnbull?'

'Gather he assaulted you.'

'Tried to.' There's a brass kettle on the hob. Looks like a proper gas job too. Has everyone got one apart from me? Either way, I'm not getting that tea, spit or not. Probably not a bad thing as tea ups my pish rate to every ten minutes. She leans back against the sink and runs a hand through her hair. 'One night I was coming home late from work, and there was a lot of shouting. I came up here, baton out, and he was off his nut, ranting about something. Chemtrails and melting steel beams and secret space programmes and all sorts of crazy nonsense.'

'Ranting at *you*?'

'Nah. I didn't know the guy, but... I attempted to calm him down, but he tried to punch me. Missed, so I overpowered him and arrested him.'

'You do him for it?'

'Last I heard, he pled guilty and got off with a caution and a fine.'

'Ever see him again?'

She shrugs. 'Not really.'

'So you don't know the boy?'

'I never really see my neighbours. There's an old man on the top floor, but that's about it.'

'Sounds like someone dodging the question to me...'

'Listen, Sergeant, I've lived here for ten years now. I bought this place and it was fine for me at the time, but nine of those long years has been trying to move. It's hard to afford anything else but I can now, finally. This is a one-bedroom flat in a block of five- and six-bedroom student places, all rammed in like sardines for eight months of the year where they're getting drunk and making a racket and pissing on the stairs. Then one month of studying, more bedlam, then some peace over the summer until they're rented out during the festival and it's *worse*. I'm sick fed up of it.'

'Don't really buy him just attacking you, though.'

'I'm not asking you to buy anything. It happened. He got arrested, charged and prosecuted for it. End of.'

'The boy's dead.'

She gasps and the cat shoots off like a banshee. The cunt scratches my leg as he goes. 'Jesus Christ. How did he die?'

'Found him at the supermarket this morning.'

'The Ashworth's?'

Got her. 'How did you know that?'

She's blushing. Won't look at us. 'I must've seen his uniform or something.'

'Right. Sharon, see, in our old annual appraisals, I used to recommend you learnt to cover up your blushing. Make sure you take a sip of water or something to think through what you're going to say before you blurt it out. If I was a fuckin' defence lawyer, I'd tear your case wide open and my client would be walking out that fuckin' door.'

'Brian, what are you trying to say?'

'That you knew the boy, didn't you? And in the biblical sense too.'

'Get out!'

'You split up from Scott, looking for a bit of greasy ramrod action, so he—'

'Shut up!' She grabs my wrists and presses hard, makes us squeal like a pig. 'Get the fuck out of my flat!'

But I'm not shifting, not even with that burning pain on my skin. 'What the fuck are you hiding from—'

She fuckin' punches us in the gut.

And I can't help myself but let out a really big fart.

6

CULLEN

Cullen sipped machine coffee and looked out of the window across the St Leonard's car park, over to Salisbury Crags, with Arthur's Seat looming in the background. 'You won't have missed the coffee.'

Angela was letting the steam waft up her face. 'Still tastes like warmed-up bleach.'

A gnarly-faced man passed through the fire doors in the corridor and walked over to them. He thrust out a hand, his nails dark with dirt like he was a keen gardener. Or just a manky git. 'Chris Leslie. I'm Mr Searle's attorney.'

'DI Cullen.' He reluctantly shook his hand. 'Not had the pleasure.'

'Are you married?'

'No.'

'Well, that'd explain it.' Leslie grinned wide. 'I'm a divorce lawyer.'

Not the kind of solicitor Cullen was used to dealing with, then. 'I wasn't aware that Mr Searle had asked for legal supervision, but he might need someone with more experience of criminal defence.'

'I'm helping a friend. These are trying times, so we'll all have to hunker down and get on with it.' Leslie pushed past Angela and entered the interview room.

Cullen let the door shut. 'We'll give them a few minutes. How you doing?'

'First day back. I'd say I've missed this, but...' Angela shook her head, spraying her loose ponytail around. 'You wanting me to lead in there?'

'If you're okay doing that.'

'Anyone ever tell you how much of a dickhead you are?'

'Pretty much everyone I meet, aye.'

Angela laughed. 'Never change, Scott.' She looked him up and down, then swallowed like she was going to say something but thought better of it. 'Right, I'll get the tape started.'

'We haven't used tape since I've been here.'

'See what I mean about you being a dickhead?' She pushed into the room.

Cullen finished his coffee alone. She was right about it tasting like bleach, but at least it had lost the temperature, so now it was just lukewarm bleach. The presence of a divorce lawyer meant they could push Searle hard, but the problem was they didn't have much to go on, just the word of a grieving father.

Hard to explain the "Evil Scotsman" message.

Hard to explain the yellow stickers.

Someone knew, all right, and Cullen had seen plenty more stupid reasons for killing. He pushed into the interview room.

Angela leaned forward, closer to the foam-tipped microphones in the middle of the table. 'DI Scott Cullen has entered the room.'

He took the seat next to her, sitting back, arms folded, his suit jacket creasing.

Angela flicked through her notebook. 'Thanks for appearing here, Mr Searle.'

Searle didn't fill her pause, just sat there. He was sweating like he was in midday Spanish sun, dots of perspiration on his forehead and all over his bald skull, damp patches under his armpit, darkening the orange polo shirt to a rusty brown.

'When my colleague here spoke to you earlier, you were more worried about covering yourself, deflecting suspicion, than expressing grief. Why was that?'

'Not sure what to say here.' Searle looked at his lawyer. 'Listen, when the cops show up, it's effing stressful.'

'In what way?'

'Well. I found Have a Phil there and...' Searle scratched at his neck. 'And you're asking me if I had anything to do with it.'

'And did you?'

'No!'

She gave him some more space, and chanced a look at Cullen, but he just nodded to continue. 'What does "Evil Scotsman" mean to you?'

'Eh?'

'The message on the floor.'

'Right. No idea.'

'None? Really?'

'No! Why would I?'

'What about the yellow stickers?'

'What about them? You think I know anything about this?'

'We gather you were making his life hell.'

'Eh? Who told you that?'

Angela sat back, arms folded again, just like Cullen so they were presenting a united front. 'Interesting.'

'What is?'

'Well, again, you didn't deny it. You asked who told us. That's very interesting to me.'

'Look, I've no idea who killed Phil so you're wasting your time with me.'

'From what we gather, you kept Phil back after his shift, knowing he'd miss his lectures.'

'No, I didn't. And besides, that's company policy.'

'What, making staff miss lectures?'

'No! I have to make sure nobody's stealing anything. Every employee is subject to a mandatory search at the end of their shift.'

'Unpaid?'

'Well, aye, but listen to me. It's company policy. I don't agree with the policy and just have to enforce whatever nonsense head office force on us.'

'I gather the check is usually one minute, maybe two.'

'Aye.'

'But he's supposed to finish at half past eight, correct?'

'Half five to half eight, aye.'

'But you were holding him back upwards of fifteen minutes.'

'Come on... Look, the cleaner and... and some other staff clock off then.'

'But given Mr Turnbull had to make it to a lecture at nine o'clock, surely you'd—'

'He was always last to join the queue. Not my fault.'

'But given his need to get down to George Square by nine, you could've—'

'He should've had a car.'

Angela let him simmer for a bit. 'But he had a bike. It's a good twenty-minute cycle to the university buildings from here. Meaning he'd have to pedal extra hard to get there, meaning he'd have to take riskier roads, putting himself at danger.'

'I don't know what you're getting at.'

'It seems like you wanted him to suffer, maybe teach him a lesson.'

'Of course I didn't!' Searle was pleading with Cullen now, but Cullen was giving him nothing back. 'Look, those effing...' He snarled out a sigh. 'Head office insist that we check all staff when they clock off. And they insist we do it in a specific order. Guards and cleaners first as they've got the most to gain from nicking stuff. Not my fault that Phil was always last in the queue. Besides, if he hated this job so badly, he could've got another one.'

Cullen leaned over to whisper in Angela's ear, 'Have we spoken to the guard?'

'Bain did, I think.'

'Right.' And the little creep was still avoiding Cullen.

Searle seemed like a petty little man, angry with the world, and his place in it. Whether he was just a malicious jobsworth or a murderer was another matter.

'Take us through your movements last night, Mr Searle.'

Searle looked at Cullen, his eyelids twitching. 'I already did.'

'Then it won't be too difficult to remember, will it?'

'Look I was with Chris here.' He thumbed at his lawyer. 'We've got a divorce hearing next week. Doing preparation, yadda yadda.'

A cast-iron alibi. Maybe. 'Sir, I'm going to need to ask you to leave.'

'What?'

'You're now involved in this case, so you can't offer legal support to Mr Searle.'

'Right.' Leslie gave Searle a look that read "I'm sorry".

Cullen leaned in to Angela. 'Can you get to the bottom of his alibi, please?'

'Sure.' She led him out into the corridor.

'DC Caldwell and Chris Leslie have left the room.' Cullen

sat there with Searle, just the two of them and the digital recorder. 'How long were you there for?'

'Two hours.'

'You didn't think to mention this earlier.'

'I'd just found a dead body!'

'You told us you got the bus home.'

Searle shook his head.

'What did you do after?'

'I don't know!'

'Earlier, you told us—'

'The Liverpool game, aye. I watched that.'

'And you couldn't prove you were at home.'

'What about if you checked my phone?'

'Your phone isn't part of you, sir. You could've left it at home, for instance, while you travelled to the supermarket to murder Mr Turnbull.'

'Is this a joke?'

'This is very serious, sir.'

Searle scratched at his stubble. 'Listen, I was drinking on my own, okay? Six cans of Brew.'

'Brew?'

'Carlsberg Special Brew.'

The tramp's friend. At least eight percent. Six cans was enough to get anyone where they wanted to go. No wonder he couldn't remember the football or his divorce hearing. 'Anyone who can vouch for you?'

His scratching increased. 'I probably texted some abuse to my ex-wife. Or hate posted on Facebook about her. Maybe on Twitter. You name it.'

Again, it all came back to his mobile. 'We might need to take your phone into evidence.'

'Come on, man, that's my life.'

'All the same.'

'Can't you just get the calls and that off the network?'

'We will, but we need the source machine to verify it.'

With a huff, Searle reached into his pocket and passed his phone over. 'I want a receipt.'

'I'll get you one.' Cullen bagged it up. Not a fancy model, but good enough to allow WhatsApp and Facebook and Twitter. And to track his every movement.

The door opened wide and DCI Colin Methven stood there, his wild eyebrows like antennas. He jerked his head out into the corridor and disappeared behind the closing door.

Cullen leaned over. 'Interview suspended at one fifteen.' He pressed stop. 'I won't be long.' He left the room and stormed out into the corridor.

Methven was shaking his head, even before Cullen had spoken. 'Purple sodding buggery.'

Never a good sign. 'What's up, sir?'

'Good to have DC Caldwell back.'

'Isn't it just.' Cullen raised his eyebrows. 'Did you speak to Super—'

'Yes, he's not related to this Turnbull.'

'Well, that's a relief.'

Methven nodded slowly.

'That all, sir?'

'No.' Methven huffed. 'DCS Carolyn Soutar called on me to advise on a case in Dundee, as you know. I worked in Grampian for a number of years and had to go down to Bonnie Dundee on a number of occasions. But then Carolyn gets a call and DS Bain is...'

Cullen got that familiar plunging in his gut. Time was it would've been waiting for a ridiculous bollocking from Bain over nothing, but now it was a ridiculous bollocking *because of* Bain. 'What's he done now, sir?'

'Where is he?'

'Last I heard, he was at the supermarket, leading the staff interviews.'

'So why the hell has Carolyn got a call complaining about his behaviour?'

Cullen tried to swallow but his throat was tight. 'I've no idea, sir.'

'And this is precisely what I've been talking to you about. He's toxic and you need to keep him on a tight leash.'

'Okay, I'll sort this out, sir. Can you tell me what he's done?'

7

BAIN

Changed days, I tell you.

These forensics boys—SOCOs to me and you, CSIs to arseholes like Sundance—have a much shiter room than they used to have down at Leith Walk. Half the fuckin' size for starters, meaning all their gear is rammed in tight, so it's much harder to spot the fuckers when you need to chivvy them up.

Still nobody here, so I take a seat behind Anderson's desk and adjust the levers until it's just right. Trouble is, I can't get it just right. Fuckin' nightmare this. No chance I can get it back to where it was either. Bugger it. I stand up again and lug my bag over my shoulder. The bargains in that place today, I swear. Cracking dinner tonight, I tell you.

The door opens and Anderson's standing there, stroking his goatee like the machines here are powered by a wanker rubbing his facial hair. He clocks my approach, though, and he shites his pants. Looks like he's thinking of making a run for it, but nobody gets away from me that easily.

'There you are.'

'Aye, here I am.' He's half turned away, pretending to check the nearest machine for something, but the fuckin' thing isn't even on. 'What's up?'

'Wondering how you're getting on, Jimbo. Hoping there's some crucial wee piece of information you can share with me.'

'I'll share it with your boss, not you.'

'Come on, Jimbo, we go back a long way.'

'Aye, and if I want to keep my pension, I'll need to side with the management here, not you.'

Prick. 'Remember how long we've been working together for.'

His eyes narrow and he gets the fuckin' message. I know where the bodies are buried and he knows what I know. He lets out a gasping sigh. 'Brian, I'm backed up. Seven cases, all needing DNA profiles yesterday.'

'But you're working on it?'

'My team are.' Anderson hits some buttons on the console in front of him, though maybe it's a panic switch for when he's outclassed by someone far superior to him. 'What are you working on, Brian?'

'I'm management, as you know. Got my lads up at the supermarket, speaking to people while I drill down to the relevant detail.'

'You're cooking something up, aren't you?'

'Why would you say that?'

'Because I know you.'

'You want in on my scheme, don't you?'

'You'll have to tell me first.'

'Nae danger!'

'So you are cooking something up. You never change, do you?'

'Why should I change? I'm the—'

'SERGEANT!'

Fuck me hard and fast, but Sundance is charging across the lino towards us, fists clenched like he's finally going to strike out at us. Fuckin' magic if he did. Been a few times I've almost had the prick, but if he punched us... Oof. Maybe I should be using that angle, just goad the cunt until he snaps.

'What's up?'

'Come here.' He grabs my jacket and pulls us away from Anderson, though the goateed fud is listening in on this. Like a nice radio drama for the boy. Maybe a podcast. Sundance leads me out into the corridor like I'm a wee dog, then into a meeting room. 'What are you thinking?'

'You don't want to know what I'm thinking, Scotty Boy.' I dump my bag on the desk. 'It'll turn your insides—'

'Listen to me! I was interviewing a suspect and DI Methven bashed down the door. Turns out you'd been upsetting people. After I warned you.'

'You'll need to be a bit more specific here on account of everyone getting offended by the most stupid fuckin' thing these days.'

He's fuckin' raging here, his face is almost the same purple as his tie. 'You didn't think to mention it to me?'

'Didn't want it to be a dead end, Scott.'

'Who told you?'

'DC Gordon got it off someone there.'

'Elvis...'

'See, I suppose it's behind his back but you're okay calling him—'

'I'm not in the fucking mood, okay?' Sundance looks like he's going to swing for us. Just bring it! 'If there's anyone round here going to speak to DI McNeill, it should be me. Okay?'

'Come on, it's not like you never ran off on a wee cowboy—'

'Shut up!' His shouting gets Anderson's deep attention

through two shut doors. The bearded fanny is looking right at us. Doesn't even turn away like any normal person would, either.

Ah, perfect. Usually when two cops go at it, there's never a witness but that fud hates Sundance as much as me. Time to turn up the fuckin' heat. 'I'm serious. I didn't think you'd want to see her after she—'

'Brian, I'm in charge of this case, okay? I'm your boss and when you or your team gets actionable intel, you make sure I'm the first person you tell. Okay?'

'Keep your knickers on, Sund—'

'I'm warning you. You're on the verge of an action contract.'

Fuckin' prick. 'You obviously weren't listening to me, earlier. I've got friends in high places.'

'I don't care if it's the First Minister or Jesus Christ. Nobody will save you.'

'You're saying Detective Chief Superintendent Carolyn Soutar can't save me?' Of course I've got a few wee things up my sleeve on that score.

But it just bounces off the cunt. 'Brian, take a long hard look at yourself. You're about to get booted back to being a constable. Nobody is saving you.'

'You want to take that risk, Sundance?'

He seems to think about it, not that thinking's his strong suit. Then he goes over to the door and opens it. 'I do, aye. I've tried warning you nicely. I've even stuck up for you when nobody else would. So here you go, nastily. If you fuck anything else up, you're getting demoted.' He thinks he means it too. Thinks he has the power. 'You'll be lucky to still be a cop once they're finished with you.'

'They?'

'DCI Methven is gunning for you.' His mouth's wide open and he's pointing down the corridor. 'Right now, I need you to prove that you can do what you're told.'

I pick up my bag off the table and wander over to him. 'I'll go and apologise to DI McNeill, Scott.' Aye, and maybe get her to drop herself in it when it comes to taking that boy's todger. 'Sorry.'

'No, you won't. You'll get back to the supermarket and manage the officers there. I'll sort it out with Sharon.'

8

CULLEN

Cullen wandered up from the Cowgate, still fizzing from the confrontation with Bain.

Where did he get off?

Cullen knew he could be a cheeky bastard at the best of times, especially at the worst of times, but Bain... Time was, Cullen would at least ask, then when he was told no, do it anyway. Bain didn't even ask, just went ahead.

His friend in high places too: DCS Soutar. She wasn't exactly the biggest fan of Cullen, but at least she knew him from when he was a DC. And his recent rise to Acting DI must have been at least with her knowledge, if not explicit approval. So he was fine.

Wasn't he? If Methven was the sponsor of his recent rise, he needed to prove it. And test it.

Cullen turned the corner and stepped under the World's

End Close sign into the dank alleyway. That familiar pong of beery urine mixed with moulding bin bags. The intercom was still smashed, possibly had even been fixed in the interim, maybe a couple of times, so he powered up the stairs and knocked on the door.

Through the wood, Dido was playing a full blast, that song Eminem sampled. At least he knew Sharon was home. Just wasn't answering the door.

He thumped it again, harder this time, giving it his policeman's knock.

And it worked. She opened the door, eyes wide and scowling. She looked well, had even put on some healthy weight, and her new haircut suited her. 'Scott?'

After everything that had passed between them, he still smiled when he saw her. 'Here to apologise, Sharon.'

'You took your sweet time.'

'Not about me. About Bain.'

'Right.' She stepped back and opened the door wide. 'You better come in, then.'

Cullen took a deep breath before venturing in. The place hadn't changed much, but she'd been burning candles, vanilla and cinnamon, probably to ward off the spirit of Bain.

Shit, he'd given them to her as a present for Valentine's day a couple of years ago.

She was in the kitchen, pouring out two cups of tea. 'Perfect timing. It's just brewed.'

'Thanks.' The bedroom and living room were filled with brown boxes. 'You're moving?'

'Nice observation there, Sherlock. Yes, I'm finally moving.'

'You know you can pay people to do that for you.'

She looked up, and it was enough to stop Cullen from progressing it any further.

'Ma-wow!' As if on cue, Fluffy stood in the doorway, bellowing at Cullen.

He crouched down and held out a finger for the cat to rub. Which the little sod actually did. He did his little dance, usually reserved for Sharon only, coiling his tail tight and zigzagging it. 'He seems well.'

'He almost died, Scott.'

'What?'

'Had a condition where his bladder was full of calcium stones. He couldn't pee.'

'Christ. You should've told me.'

'Should I.' A statement, not a question. 'You still take milk?'

'Nah. Drink it black these days. Haven't had milk for... ooh months now.'

'Suit yourself.' She passed him a cup, but kept her distance. 'Why the hell have you kept Bain on?'

Cullen hid behind his mug. Kept his gaze on Fluffy, prancing around at Sharon's feet.

'I heard Methven gave you the opportunity to get rid of him.'

'That what you heard?' Cullen laughed. 'Methven said if I got rid of him, I'd lose a sergeant position in my team. As hard as it is these days, working these cases with only one sergeant isn't much fun and Chantal's away on a bloody hen week. Craig's even mo—'

'Even so. Having Bain must be like a minus two to your headcount. Sometimes it's better to have an empty seat than let him sit in one.'

'I know. Look, me and Crystal have agreed to get rid of him once I've hired a replacement. There's a job posted, I'm interviewing. Once it's filled...' Cullen made a slit throat gesture.

'Believe it when I see it.'

'He didn't tell me he was coming here.'

'Right, so if you'd known, then *you* would've been the one insulting me?'

Cullen laughed. 'We're not even going out any more, and you're still giving me shit?' He knew he shouldn't have said it.

But she didn't react like he expected. She ran a hand down his arm. 'Scott, I'm just trying to help, okay? I worked directly for him for six years. He's toxic. If he's not making an arse of something, he'll be plotting against you.'

Cullen took a drink of tea. Oily and fragrant. 'Well, I'm equal to whatever he throws at me.'

'Your funeral.' Sharon looked away, sipping her tea. 'How's Yvonne?'

So she knew, then? 'Eve's fine.'

'You've got a pet name for her?'

Cullen shrugged, losing himself in his teacup.

'Are you living together?'

'No.'

'As in, no never or not yet?'

'Living apart. Seeing each other a few times a week. I've got a flat in Leith.'

'Near Craig's?'

'Actually Craig's. Subletting it.'

'He's moved in with Chantal?'

'You didn't know?'

'We don't speak any more.'

'Right. Well. I don't know if me and Eve are serious or not.'

'I thought I was in love with you.' She held his gaze, sipping her tea. 'Don't fuck this up, Scott. And get rid of Bain.'

Nice change of subject. 'What did he say to you?'

'How much do you know?'

'Enough.'

'Right, well, he insinuated that I was shagging that kid who died.'

'Sharon, you know I need to ask, right?'

'You shouldn't ask someone that who's holding a hot mug of tea.' She held the cup high. 'Of course I wasn't.'

'And there's no evidence to suggest you were?'

'*Scott.*'

'Okay, okay. So this kid attacked you?'

'Tried to. I mean, he was wasted. Like even worse than you when you pissed in that sink.'

'Don't remind me.'

'Can't do the time, don't do the crime.'

'Weird how he lived downstairs.'

'Not when you were here, Scott. He's only been in since the start of September.'

'How do you know?'

'Bumped into him and a flatmate as they were lugging in this massive DJ sound system. Knew it was going to be a disaster. And it was.'

'What are the kids down there like?'

'Not sure. You know I like to keep myself to myself.'

'Smart move.' Cullen finished his tea. 'Look, I'm really sorry about Bain.'

'You need to get rid of him, Scott. Mark my words.'

'Okay, okay. Look, I'm interviewing Craig's old sergeant tomorrow night. On the sly.'

'So Bain's cards *are* marked?' She looked like she was struggling to hide the smile. 'Thank god.'

'I'll put in a recommendation to send him to Bathgate.'

'No you bloody won't.'

Cullen put the cup in the sink. Fluffy started circling his feet. 'I'll see you around.'

'Wait a sec.' She took a sip of her own tea, eyes narrowing. 'Look, Bain coming here jostled a few memories, okay?'

'About us?'

She was blushing. 'Snogging downstairs, like we used to. Desperate to get up here.' She shut her eyes. 'It made me remember something. I can't swear on it, but I think I saw Phil with a woman, at least a couple of times. Kissing downstairs like they were in a hurry to get home.'

'You mean, like a girlfriend?'

'I do, but she was a lot older than him.'

9

BAIN

Where the fuck does he get off?

Sundance, I made that prick.

And this arsehole in the Vectra just ahead of me, thinking he's the Boy. Alloy wheels and lowered suspension. Still his fuckin' dad's motor, even if the imbecile's welded a spoiler on the back.

I'll show him who's the boss. I kick down to second and floor it, weaving the duchess around the wanker, giving him a polite wave, head tilted, as I pass and—

SHITE.

A fuckin' bus is hurtling right towards me.

Brakes on, squeal and I slide back in behind the Vectra. The bus hisses past. Fuckin' close one. Prick should've let me out earlier, so he's getting a pounded horn for his trouble. Even has the cheek to flip me the bird, as the Yanks would say.

Just as well I'm at Ashworth's or I'd pull him over and ruin his fuckin' day. Probably no end of shite he's hiding from the long arm of the fuckin' law.

I pull up at the outer locus. The wee fanny's still clutching his clipboard like he's important. I shove my warrant card against the glass and pull past without signing. He can do some work for a change.

Still, it's nice to have my choice of parking spaces for once, so I park across two disabled bays without the fear of some jobsworth coming over and shouting at us. I get out of the duchess and stretch. Might be brass monkeys, but it's a braw day. Nice and bright. Swear when I got up this morning, I thought it was going to—

What the hell are they up to?

My heart's fuckin' racing as I plough over there.

That manager—Searle or something—is locked in a heated battle with those arseholes Sundance saddled us with: Hunter and Buxton. Livid too, jabbing his finger at Hunter. Bad move, by all accounts. As much of a dick as Hunter is, I've seen him take down boys even bigger than him, and in fuckin' seconds too.

'What's going on here?'

Searle swivels round and clocks us. Takes him a few seconds before he moves, but he gets in my face now. Christ, he stinks like a microbrewery. Second-hand booze is seeping out of every pore. 'I need to open up and she won't honour that.'

He switches his focus to this tiny wee lassie I've only just spotted. Uniformed sergeant, and kind of cute with it. She's got two or three coats on, though, and it's not *that* cold, is it?

Some boys only like a man in uniform, so I give her a "relax, doll, Brian's in charge" look, then get in his face. 'Listen, sir, you found a body in there.' He's inches from my neb now, meaning I'm fighting hard against looking away from the smelly bastard. 'My job is to find who murdered him. My colleagues are still in there analysing forensics, so you'll be lucky if you can open later this week let alone today.'

Boy's fuming, like he can already see a difficult conversation with his bosses playing out, and all the cards he's holding are pish ones. Aye, join the club, pal. 'This *week*?'

'For clarity, I mean Monday morning, aye, and I'd be doubtful of that.'

'Christ.'

I wrap my arm around his shoulders and lead him away. 'Listen, I appreciate you giving us access to the back store CCTV footage, but have you given us access to the rest of it yet?'

'No, I've just had to attend a police interview.'

Sundance, Sundance, Sundance... 'Sorry to hear that, sir.'

'No, I want them to find Phil's killer.'

'So, can you give DC Hunter here access to the video?'

'Sure.' He nods and leads the big bastard inside. Buxton shuffles off after them, more like a spare part than ever.

Means I can let out a deep breath. But I can't take it back in because Elvis is on us. Where did he come from? He points at Hunter as he takes the boy back to the front door. 'Cheers, Sarge.'

'For what?'

'Giving us a break from that kind of rubbish.'

I fix him with that look. 'Don't kid yourself, son. You're helping interview all the customers Hunter and Buxton find.'

'Right.'

'And in the meantime, I need you to speak to the other employees.'

'Already done that.'

'Well done.' And that bird is charging away from the store. A wee bit of me can just picture her on the blower to her boss, then any old shite coming back to bite my arse. And I need to keep all my trump cards in my pocket for use against Sundance. 'Who's that?'

'Her?' Elvis scowls. 'Lauren Reid. Craig's old boss. Why?'

'Just want to check who's about to grass on us.' But something in his frown makes us stop. 'What is it?'

'The cleaner fucked off before we could finish up with him.'

'What exactly hadn't you finished?'

'Well, Cullen had me asking him about his key.'

What the hell is this clown on about? 'His *key*?'

Elvis steps away from us and looks at us side on. 'Aye, he'd left it behind at home. No forced entry, so you know the drill.'

'And then he fucked off?'

Another step away from the boy. 'Aye.'

'Fuckin' find him!'

10

CULLEN

Cullen knocked on the door and waited. 'You know you shouldn't be here, right?' He glanced at Sharon. 'I can handle this.'

'Really?' She looked around at him. 'I don't see Budgie or Craig Hunter or anyone. You need two cops.'

'You're off duty.'

'Got my warrant card.'

She was right and Cullen felt like such an idiot. Maybe his ascendancy to DI had been too quick; she'd had years as a DS versus barely three for him, on and off. 'Angela Caldwell's on her way.'

'She's back?'

'First day.'

'My god. How's she coping?'

'Well as can be expected, I suppose. Let's just see how this goes.'

The door opened and a bulky guy stood there, his thick beard tucked into the neck of a muscle shirt. Cullen clocked Sharon checking him out. 'I've heard the good news, thank you very—'

'Police, sir.' Cullen blocked the doorway with his foot and held up his warrant card. 'Does Philip Turnbull live here?'

'Uh, yeah. Listen, I've got a lecture in like ten minutes.' Hard to place his accent. Could be American, maybe.

'We should do this inside.'

'You aren't getting in here without a goddamn warrant.' It wasn't American. Maybe European?

'This is a delicate matter, sir. Mr Turnbull is dead.'

He sighed. 'Come in, then.'

That was it? Didn't even swallow or anything.

He stepped aside to let Cullen and Sharon past.

But Cullen had seen that trick so many times, so he let the not-so-big lump go first.

The place was like any number of student flats Cullen had been in over the years, as a student himself, as a cop or... for other reasons. Nocturnal ones. A grotty kitchen, with posters on the wall advertising bands, TV shows, games, all stuff Cullen didn't recognise. Christ, he must be getting old. A massive telly sat opposite a battered couch that must be a haven for dust mites.

'What's your name, sir?'

'Josef Sarmast. It's Norwegian.' He flexed a giant bicep and frowned at Sharon. 'I know you, right?'

She nodded. 'I live upstairs.'

Something churned deep in Cullen's guts, something he didn't like. He got between them. 'How many of you live here?'

'Eh, five of us. The rest are at lectures.'

'Were you close?'

'Three of us are. Me, Ross and Bickett have lived here since second year. This is our third year. We found Jack and Dave last year. Dave moved out, and Philip moved in at the start of this year.'

'And did you speak to him much?'

'I mean, we spoke to him, but he kept himself to himself. Just saw him when he was making his toast and beans.'

'Toast and beans?'

'Porridge for breakfast, toast and beans for lunch and dinner. Every single day. He said he was a vegetarian, but I'm not sure a tin of beans counts, does it?'

Sharon smiled at him. 'You look like you know about nutrition?'

'I work out.' He shrugged. 'Phil didn't.'

Cullen tried to get his attention, but he only had eyes for Sharon. 'Does the "Evil Scotsman" mean anything to you?'

That got a look. Josef rolled his eyes too. 'It's a song he sang when he was drunk.'

'A song?'

'I mean, he was drunk a lot. I don't drink, work out every day. But he drank pretty much constantly. Like Fresher's Week all the time.'

'I've never heard of that song.'

'It's supposed to be by Billy Connolly but it's just some guy, and it's to the tune of an old Alanis Morissette song. It's really rude and stuff. He kept playing it to Ross, but it's not very funny and it's pretty sick.'

'Anyone get particularly offended by it?'

'Nah, bro. We're all polite as.'

Cullen gave him a nod. 'Do you know if he was romantically involved with anyone?'

'Not that I'm aware of, no.'

'When he was drunk, you ever see or hear him coming back late with anyone?'

'His room's the other end from mine, so no.'

'No women coming back with him?'

'Bro, I can't help you. Sorry.'

He was right. As much as Cullen wanted to push, he was facing a brick wall here. 'What was he studying?'

'Well, business.'

'Why did you say "well"?'

'Because Ross and Bickett were on the same course as him. Kind of how they met him, but like they're not his friends. A few weeks ago, Phil stopped going to his lectures.'

'What happened?'

'The way I hear it, there were allegations about him and a university member of staff. She was suspended, pending an investigation.'

11

BAIN

One good side about all this pish is that I don't need to fuckin' queue to get the yellow items. The canteen might be empty, but my table's nice and full. Some sandwiches, big bag of own-brand crisps and two tins of WakeyWakey. Lunch of champions, if that's a thing. I take my time finishing the second BLT, even tastier than the first, and swallow it down with some energy drink, ready to pep myself up for this call. I put the phone to my ear and listen to the ringing.

But I'm facing up to the fuckin' bad news here. Sundance, cheeky prick, thinking he can tell me what to do. Arsehole is bringing a knife to a fuckin' nuclear war, I tell you. Just need to launch my ICBMs, then detonate the warheads on the cunt.

Here goes.

'This is Carolyn. Sorry I can't take your call just now, but please leave a message and I'll get back to you. Alternatively, if you call my office, Elaine will help. Thanks and take care.'

Fuck's sake. I hit dial again.

'This is Carolyn. Sorry I can't—'

Right. I've got this. Her office number is next to her moby so I jab a finger on that. Let's see if she'll answer *this* call, eh?

'Carolyn Soutar's office, Elaine speaking.'

'Elaine!' Try to leave it all friendly, let her make the move, but she doesn't fill the gap. 'It's Brian. Carolyn there?'

'Ah, Superintendent Masson. I'll see if she's available.'

'No, it's Brian *Bain*.'

'Ah.' Her pause suggests she remembers all that Miss Moneypenny flirting over the years. 'Well, I'm afraid that Carolyn is in meetings all day.'

'Wait a sec, you just said you'll see if she's available.'

'Yes. I was thinking you were Detective Superintendent Brian Masson. You'll be aware of the incident in Dundee, yes?'

'No, but I really need to speak to her.'

'Brian, there's a serious incident in Tayside just as the country is approaching lockdown.' She's talking now like she does recognise us.

'Elaine, tell Carolyn she wants to answer the phone to me.'

'Sergeant, I shall give her your regards the first chance I get, but this incident is taking up all her time. Now, unless you've got intel on either matter, then I suggest you clear the line.'

She doesn't give me a choice, just bumps me off it.

Fuck. Sake.

I tap Dundee into Google but nothing much is coming up in the news. Keeping whatever's going down there a secret. I know a few journos who'd like that inside track, though, boys and girls who'd pay top fuckin' dollar for just a sniff.

But I'm an honest man. Unlike Sundance.

Prick. I'm going to double down on what I've already got planned for him.

Speak of the devil and he shall appear. Hunter the Cunter is standing there, scowling at us.

I stuff another handful of crisps in my mouth and fuck me the vinegar is fuckin' strong. 'What's up, Big Man?'

He stays there, holding a laptop like he's my old man and hasn't the foggiest on how to get *Grandstand* to play on it, like they even fuckin' show that any more. 'I've got the CCTV.'

'Excellent.' I swipe all the shite onto the floor and gesture at a seat. 'Pull up a pew.'

He does but he's looking like I've sneezed all over the table and he's going to catch that fuckin' bug off it. 'Okay, so the bad news first.'

'Shitload of that going around.'

'Excuse me?'

'Nothing.'

'Right, well, there's no CCTV for the store room.'

'Should there be?'

'Aye.' Hunter swivels the laptop round to me, but I've no idea what it's supposed to signify. He taps the screen. 'Someone's turned off the camera.'

'And here's me thinking you'd swoop in like a hero and solve this.'

'Wish I could.'

I peer at the screen and there's a hand reaching up to cover the lens. 'So you mentioned something about good news. I take it you've found whose hand that is?'

'No, but...' He takes the laptop back and does some one-finger typing. Honestly, my old man has more tech savvy than this fud. 'I've found footage of the guys waiting for the pricing gun last night.'

'Vultures.'

'Eh?'

'That's what the boss here calls them.' I shift over to have a peek at the screen, playing a scene not unlike a nature documentary as the pack of vultures launch themselves at a coyote just as it pops its clogs.

A few supermarket employees hanging around like they're pretending to do their jobs, and about ten customers, all men. Good work, boys!

Hunter points at one. 'Watch him.'

Skinny guy, dark hair but balding like he's got one of those monk things. A tonsure? That's it! The boy's acting well shifty, likes. Hanging around the cake section, looking over his shoulder as if he's up to something snide.

An employee appears and he's even shiftier now.

Hunter prods the screen again. 'That's Phil Turnbull.'

I pause it and squint but these peepers aren't so good these days. 'Sure?'

'Positive.'

The Phil boy says something to the other one, and he fucks off sharpish. Phil follows him over and picks up a massive cake, shaking his head.

'What's going on there, Craig?'

'Need to speak to the manager to see if he knows, but it looks like the guy's switched price stickers from another product to that.'

Genius! Why the hell have I never tried that ruse? 'Anything to support that theory?'

'Not yet.'

'Okay, so you got anything else?'

'Aye.' He does some more old-man typing and brings up another video. Looks like the adjacent aisle, bread rather than cakes. 'This guy here.'

And it's obvious who he means. Boy with a hook nose and a cheeky grin on his face. Real wide bastard by the looks of him. Basket full of meat and other products. He picks up a loaf of Hovis from the shelf, but it looks like someone's shat on his shoes. What a face, all twisted up with rage as he looks around. He starts off across the aisle, shouting at someone off camera.

And Young Phil appears, looking a bit nervous. Says something to the boy.

The shopper shakes the bread at him, says something else.

And there's some movement from the right. A security guard, the same twenty-stone hoofer Elvis spoke to earlier, but big enough to frighten the bread bastard off. He dumps his basket and hotfoots it out of there.

'What in the name of the wee man was going on there?'

'Looks like he was threatening him.'

'Those are promising, Craig.' I tear open the bar of chocolate. Nowhere near its date but fuck it, nobody's looking. 'Any idea how we can track them down?'

Hunter lets out a sigh he's clearly learnt from his mate, Sundance. 'Well, assuming they bought stuff in the last week, I could go through till records, find all reduced items, then use their Cashworth Member's Card to get addresses.'

'What's stopping you, then?'

12

CULLEN

George Square meant the University of Edinburgh. Half a block of lovely old Georgian townhouses, a load of Sixties monstrosities, and some turn-of-the-millennium chrome-and-glass stuff. Shouting and grinding came from the nearby square that skateboarders had commandeered years ago. No matter what the university did, they still couldn't shift them.

Cullen leaned back against his car and let out a sigh. 'Haven't been here in a while.' He remembered the business department used to be in the William Robertson building, right in a horrendous wind tunnel, but it had moved round to one of the posh old houses. Maybe it had been in David Hume Tower, one of the two giant monstrosities that blighted Edinburgh's southside skyline.

Angela was leaning against her car, shades on. 'The old alma mater, right?'

'Right. Time and a place for everything.'

'And that's called college. Yeah, yeah.'

'Sorry, Yvonne's got me watching old *South Park* episodes just now.'

'Didn't think that'd be her bag.'

'Me neither.'

'Still, Netflix and chill. Must be serious?'

'It's Amazon Prime, but yeah.' Cullen found himself smiling. He sniffed it away. 'You want to lead in here?'

'Oh, that'd be super sexy.' Angela rolled her eyes and skipped up the steps. She stabbed the button and waited, arms folded.

Cullen took his time climbing up. No messages on his phone, which meant Bain hadn't set off any more fireworks. At least none that Methven had been made aware of. 'I saw Sharon today.'

'You okay?'

'We're fine.'

'I heard she's moving.'

'Right, so you're still in touch, then.'

'One of the few who'll even speak to me.' She hit the buzzer again. 'People are *weird*.'

'They'll come round. Don't worry.'

'Just wondering if returning to this job is the right move.'

'You need a job and you're good at this one.' Cullen shrugged. 'And I'll need a sergeant once I've kicked Bain into touch.'

'Seriously?'

'Watch this space.'

The intercom rasped. 'Hello?'

'DC Caldwell here to see Professor McGarrigle?'

The door buzzed.

'See what I mean?' Cullen followed her inside. 'Bain would've just tried to blag his way in. You called ahead.'

PROFESSOR PAUL MCGARRIGLE'S office looked across George Square. Despite the cold weather, the park was full of students chatting and drinking coffee. He was a thin man with a large belly. Early forties, so his tweeds seemed a bit out of place, especially in the business studies department, where they'd pioneered that open-collar look. 'Look, I just can't talk about it.'

'But you are the head of department?'

'Correct.'

'And you won't talk to the police about these allegations.'

'It's not a police matter, so I don't have to.'

'It is now.' Cullen tossed a crime scene photo onto the massive desk. Nothing revealing, but with just enough veracity to spook the guy. 'We found his body this morning.'

McGarrigle slumped back in his chair, eyes shut. 'Shite almighty.'

Cullen motioned for Angela to give him space and time.

'Shite, shite, shite.' McGarrigle looked at them both, slowly. 'How did he die?'

'We're working on that, sir.' Angela collected up Cullen's photos. 'We need to assess whether his murder is rel—'

'*Murder*?'

She nodded. 'We believe so, yes.'

'Heavens to Betsy...'

'We need to determine if his murder was connected to what's been going on here.'

'Well, I can't comment on it as it pertains to a member of staff.'

'Sir, not only can you, but you must. This is a murder case.'

'And we're managing the matter internally. I can't divulge sensitive information like that without a warrant.'

That old chestnut.

Cullen tried to see a way out of the maze. There were a few

options he had, but all were pretty unlikely to get a truculent academic to budge, not without a court-ordered warrant. Still, the sooner he got on with it... He gave Angela a flash of his eyes and a tilt of the head. Keep at it, force him to talk. He made his way back out into the corridor.

The reception area was two desks, but only one secretary on. And scurrying back to her desk. He'd clearly interrupted her nosing in on their meeting. Late thirties, with wild curly hair.

Cullen got out his phone—still no messages—and called Methven.

'Scott, I'm in the middle of a meeting. Can I call you back?'

'Having a bit of trouble at the university, sir.'

'Edinburgh? This is what you texted me about?'

It would've been much easier if Methven had answered his phone earlier. 'Right. Seems like Philip Turnbull was on suspension. Trouble is, the head of department isn't speaking to us.'

'You need me to figure something out? Sodding hell, Scott, this isn't what I need just now.'

'You're better connected than I am.'

'Indeed.' Methven paused. Sounded like he was outside a room where a lot of people were shouting inside. 'You need a warrant, I take it?'

'Assuming you can get a friendly judge to sign one. I can be down at the courts in minutes.'

'I've got a better idea. DCS Soutar knows the chancellor. Leave it with me.'

'Thanks, sir.' Cullen smiled, though only the secretary was there to see it, and pocketed his phone.

The secretary was still looking at him. 'This about Philip Turnbull?'

Cullen took one look at the office door, deciding that Angela had it covered. Best to keep the Soutar-chancellor bombshell in his back pocket for now. He walked over and perched on the edge of the desk. 'Strange business.'

'I know.' She waved a hand over at the other desk. 'One of the many reasons why this place has gone to the dogs, not least since we moved here.'

So the spare desk was somehow connected? Cullen sat in the seat, trying to act all casual. 'But your boss is the main reason, right?'

'Tell me about it. So out of his depth. The old guy? He got Me-Tooed out of the door, golden handcuffs, no investigation. Probably why they don't want to speak to you lot.'

'Probably. Any idea what we should've been speaking to them about?'

'Nah, he was just overly touchy-feely. Old school. I didn't mind it, but Jenny thought he was a creep.' She was eyeing up the other desk, the one Cullen sat at.

'That why she's not here?'

She leaned in close. 'No, she got caught shagging a student.'

'Here?'

'Christ, what have you heard?'

'Precious little, which is the problem.' Her scowl showed Cullen he was losing her, so he leaned over to her. 'Was the student Philip Turnbull, right?'

'Right. I mean, he's okay, but it's not worth losing your job over, is it?'

'She got sacked?'

'Nah, just suspended.'

'Oh?'

'You don't know?'

'Your boss isn't talking to us.'

She shook her head. 'He's such a dick.' She patted the locked filing cabinet between them. 'Jenny got caught stealing an exam paper for her young lover.'

CULLEN PULLED up behind Angela's pool car and tried the number again.

'We're sorry but—'

Voicemail.

He pocketed his phone and looked at Jenny Black's home. A two-storey ex-council house on the city's southside. He'd lost track of the street names two turns back, but Angela had kept on going. Must be her satnav or she just knew the area.

Cullen got out onto the street. The morning's sunshine had given way to lunchtime gloom. And that wind cut right through him. 'Still can't get hold of her.'

Angela locked her car manually. Definitely a case of drawing the short straw—one of those old undercover cars designed to blend in deep in the arse end of Muirhouse. 'Any sign of her?'

Cullen checked the house again. Assuming hers was bottom-left in the block, which seemed okay judging by the number, then it looked dark as night. At midday. 'Let's see.' He walked up the path and tried the door.

The bell chimed, but no sounds came from anywhere inside.

Cullen hit dial again, and the phone inside rang until the answerphone caught it. 'Wish I had her mobile number.'

'Wish you had a plan, Scott. What's the logic here?'

'Why don't you talk me through it.'

Angela prodded the bell again. 'She shagged this kid, thinks she's going to lose her job, so she kills him. That about it?'

'When you say it out loud like that, it does seem a bit of a stretch.'

'This is just buying time until Crystal gets us a warrant, right?'

'He should be here, but he's brown nosing our boss. Why take a murder case if you're going to just delegate it all?'

'Why have a DI if you have to do all the work? Maybe he trusts you.'

Cullen laughed. 'We really need to speak to her.'

'She's not in.' A purple-faced man was standing in the small garden to the side, trying to get a handmower to do any cutting by the looks of things. 'And you can clear off.'

'Police, sir.' Angela held up her warrant card. 'When did you last see her?'

'Last night. She popped in, asking if I'd mind watering her plants. Poor thing's not been the same since her divorce. And then all this business with the young lad... Taxi took her to the airport.'

'She say where she was going?'

'Magaluf for a week. Trying to ignore it all, wasn't she?' He bent down to claw at the mower's blades. 'Had a couple of journalists snooping around earlier.'

Cullen just knew he'd have to chase a few of them down. 'You got her mobile number?'

His mower was free again. 'Afraid not.'

13

BAIN

And Caz is still fuckin' bumping my calls, isn't she? Cow. After all I've done for her. After all I've got on her?

I chuck my moby on the table and it cracks like I've broken the screen. Have to take a look at it, but the thing's tougher than I thought. Mind when I used to go through these things every few months. Should've jacked in policing and taken up industrial testing for fuckin' Nokia.

Right, no point in getting angry about this whole shitshow.

Fuck it, of course there is. I hammer out a text:

Caz I really need to speak to you ok? Bri

Fuckin' beauty of WhatsApp is you can see when it's been delivered to their phone and—BINGO—when they've read it. Those beautiful blue ticks appear, like an oasis in the desert to a man dying of thirst. Only this is no mirage. And she's starting to type.

Come on, come on, come on.

Fuckin' downside is you can see them stopping. Fuck sake.

Still, there's Elvis just popping into the canteen. Not with any of the staff, so I should probably figure out where he's got to with all the actual work.

'You found him?'

He just shrugs. 'Not yet.'

Boy doesn't seem himself. 'You okay?'

'It's... I don't know. Speaking to the public, sometimes I should just get on with checking CCTV.'

'You stupid bastard. You should keep your trap shut in future, especially when you talk to Cullen.'

'Aye, I will.'

'Seen Hunter?'

'Not for a while. He pissed off back to St Leonards, I think.'

'What's he fuckin' doing there?'

'Got a spreadsheet to look at.'

'Can't you do it for him?'

'He said Cullen told him not to let anyone help. What can I do?'

'Fuck sake. Sundance will be the death of me.'

The door swings open and Searle appears. He scans around like there's anyone other than me and Elvis in there, then waltzes over. 'Listen, have you seen DI Cullen?'

'Not for a while.' Almost smile at myself there. 'Anything I can help with?'

'Well, I've tried calling a DCI Methven, but he's not answering.'

Fuckin' class. He's moaning about Sundance to the boss! 'What was the nature of your inquiry?'

'I keep getting pressure from management in Crieff to open this place up. DI Cullen passed on DCI Methven's details. I need to get this place open!'

'That isn't going to happen.'

'I'll lose my job.'

'How about I give him a bell and see what I can do?'

Seems to pacify the boy.

Not that I'll actually do anything about it. This place is shut for the foreseeable and the daft sod needs to get used to that fact. 'Leave it with me.' So I point at the pew opposite. 'Got a few questions, if you wouldn't mind.'

The jakey bastard sighs as he collapses into the seat. 'What's up?'

I give Elvis a click of the fingers. 'Show him.'

Prick's frowning. 'Show him what?'

'The CCTV.'

'That was Craig.'

Fuckity fuck. Aha, but I took some sneaky little snapshots on the moby. 'Never mind, I'll do it myself.' So I take it out and show the boy.

Searle's a shady fucker, alright. Taking his time checking.

'You know anything about these?'

'I told your boss earlier about vultures. Yellow-item fiends.' He rests my phone on the table and sits back. Another big Sundance-level sigh. 'Phil worked some evening shifts. The last couple of hours, he scouts out which aisles need stocking the most during nightfill. He's long gone by the time we're facing up.'

'Which is what?'

Elvis is grinning at us. 'It's when they turn the labels to all face the same way.'

Searle frowns at the wee bastard. 'You worked in a supermarket?'

'Willie Low's, then Safeway, then the Ashworth's in Clermiston.'

Searle loses his grin. 'Bit weird that you worked for two supermarkets that went to the wall. Hope we're not next.'

This is all lovely stuff—never knew that about Elvis—but

c'mon tae fuck. 'Right, so what was Mr Turnbull doing in that photo?'

'Right.' Searle runs a hand across his head, then picks up my phone again. Going to regret that, he's getting his sweat all over it. He holds it up. 'This guy...' Shakes his head, like me or Elvis know. 'We get him in here all the time. The guard told me about it. What he's doing is a common trick, where these effing sods mis-price something.'

'Explain.'

'See that cake?' He's jabbing a filthy finger on my phone. 'He's got a sticker from a manky cake, marking it down from four quid to 99p—and you'd have to be *desperate* to buy that— and he's stuck it onto a four quid sirloin steak.'

'You say he's doing it all the time?'

'Right. Boy's always trying it, most times he gets away with it. Sometimes he gets caught.'

It's fuckin' genius. The more I hear about it, the more I want to try it. Reckon those self-serve tills are wide open to it in the other places.

Elvis is interested. Eyes shut, fingers steepled in front of his face. 'How does it work?'

'Not following you, bud.'

'Well, surely your tills aren't still manual?'

'What?'

'Dude, I worked in one in 1999, and they hadn't converted. It's 2020, surely you've got barcode scanners.'

'We do, but... The system is flaky as hell. If you go to Tesco or Asda, it's very detailed, so the cashier can see the tin of tomatoes they've scanned is a tin of tomatoes. And the self-service stuff, which we don't have, will show the punter what they've just scanned and not put in the bagging area.'

Bollocks. The weights would need to match. Would a cake be the same as a steak?

'So I keep telling my bosses about it, but they're very much of the "look after the pennies and the pounds look after them-selves" school. They don't want to invest in anything.'

'Jeez.'

Time to assert some bloody control here. 'Okay, so the defi-ciencies of your tills aside, do you think this boy here had any gripes against Mr Turnbull?'

'Well, Phil was the one who kept catching him. Knew what he was up to, so spotted him, then followed him at a distance, watching him do it with the security guard.'

'Any way you can find him?'

'We've not—' Searle pauses, his ugly mug all screwed up. 'Wait a sec. He bought something, at least according to the guard.'

THE GUARD WAS at least twenty stone of idiot shoved into a tiny wee cupboard by the stairs, a sagging chair in front of CCTV monitors that must've seen service in the Second World War. Shaved head, but an elaborate-as-fuck beard. And I know the boy from somewhere.

Our knees are almost touching. Christ knows how Hunter managed to sit next to him. 'You used to be a cop?'

He nods at us. 'Leith, aye. Got my twenty and got out.' More like he did something and got booted.

'What happened?'

'I collared him.' The boy taps the screen. 'Phil said the boy had a six-pack of WakeyWakey energy drink in his basket, so when I collared him by the door, the suspect denied all knowledge of the steak. Said it was nowt to do with him.'

Still got the police officer patter. Formal language, exert authority so no cunt tears your statement apart. 'What happened to the steak?'

'Couldn't sell it after it'd been out of the fridge for an inde-
terminate amount of time.'

Searle's standing in the doorway, hands in pockets. 'I
thought about frying it up for you this morning.'

Actually feel a bit sick. And a bit hungry. 'But you didn't?'

'Nah, was going to have it for my dinner.'

'We'll need to take that into evidence, sir.'

'Evidence?'

'To compare prints. DC Gordon here will add that to your
statement.'

'Okay.' Boy looks pissed off at losing all that meaty
goodness.

I focus hard on him, trying to bring him back. 'So we can
trace him through the tills?'

'Should be able to, aye.'

I click my fingers at Elvis and get him to break out of his
intellectual prayer pose. 'Can you let DC Hunter know we're on
to something?'

'Sure thing, Sarge.' He slopes off like he's just got a delivery
of craft beer.

Searle's still got my bloody phone. Hope the better half
hasn't fuckin' texted us while he's got it. I snatch if off him and
point to the screen, showing the boy shouting the odds at our
murder victim. 'Know anything about him?'

'He's a nightmare.'

'What's going on here?'

'Okay, so we've got this system where if the price on the
receipt doesn't match that on the shelf, the customer gets a
voucher. Five quid, I think. This boy's always at it.'

'Struggling to see how he'd get so angry.'

'He won't buy a loaf of bread until it's 10p, then he'll fill his
trolley. When he was on the pricing gun, Young Phil used to
play this game, reducing them from fifty to twenty, then fifteen,
then thirteen, seeing when he'd bite.'

'So he'd cottoned on to it?'

'Aye.' The guard takes over. 'Suspect he's moaning about how disgusting it is to have to pay 15p for a loaf of bread. I mean...'

'With you now.'

The guard's nodding at me. 'This boy seems like a suspect, though.'

'Agreed. Any idea where we could find him?'

'No, but he's a mate of the cleaner.'

I GET out of the duchess first. 'Why the fuck did you let him leave?'

'Like I keep telling you...' The gate squeaks as Simon Buxton opens it. 'I didn't. Hunter did.'

'Well, I don't believe you.' I jostle the English prick out of the way as I charge up the path and thump on the door.

This place is completely fucked, by the way. Falling apart. Battered old council house in the arse end of Clermiston, not that there's a better end. Maybe where the Tesco is. If I wasn't with Buxton, I'd head up there and scope out the yellow items. Starving now. Swear I got a full rotisserie chicken for 10p in there once. Gorgeous too.

Buxton's on the grass, peeking in the front room. Fuckin' hell, there's another Sundance nickname right there. Budgie. Cheeky twat has the temerity to moan about me giving people nicknames? 'He's in there.' He charges back over and thumps on the door. 'Police!'

No answer.

'Right, son. You get us in there.'

'Sure?'

'Sure.' Budgie tries the handle. The door doesn't shift. He clicks his neck twice then steps back and launches his shoulder at it, but the door opens just before he makes contact.

The big cleaner bastard's standing there, mouth hanging open, eyes like saucers full of secrets.

Buxton tumbles over the doorway and smacks into the boy, headfirst. He just bounces off him and goes down like a sack of spuds.

The cleaner boy's taking a fortnight to look around at me. 'What's going on here?'

'MY TEES!' Buxton is scrabbling round on the floor and he looks up at us and HOLY FUCK. His mouth is a bloody mess, big gaps where his front teeth used to be. 'WHERE ARE MY TEES!?'

14

CULLEN

Tommy Smith looked Cullen up and down. His grizzled face was blunted by a thick beard, way too dark for his white hair on top. 'You look like you're at a bit of a dead end there.'

'In a manner of speaking.' Cullen sat down next to him at the desk, double the size of theirs downstairs and filled with all manner of fancy-looking IT equipment. 'Need to trace a phone.'

'Aye?' Tommy cracked his knuckles and unlocked his machine. 'Got a number?'

Cullen showed his notebook.

Tommy hammered the keys and sat back while the machine did some work. 'You haven't responded to that email about my retirement bash.'

'Don't remember seeing it.'

'I sent it to your work and private emails, Scott.'

'Might be out of town.'

'Oh aye. Haven't told you the date.'

'You sent an email with no date on it?'

'Just a weekend. Anyway, we've got a big room provisionally booked for the Friday and Saturday nights. Booked a band too.'

Cullen could just see how the evening would play out. Terrible covers, spoken word, tedious disco and way too much booze. 'I'll let you know tomorrow.'

'Good man.'

'How's that trace going?'

'Slow. All the resources are devoted to this thing in Dundee.'

'Any idea what's going on up there?'

'DCI and above, Scott. Unless you're directly involved, like me. And I could tell you, but I'd have to kill you.'

'That'd be a popular move round here.'

Tommy laughed. 'Heard you've got a new bird.'

'Well, I wouldn't be so crass.'

'Course you would.' And as if by magic, Tommy's machine bleeped. 'There we go. That mobile is in Spain. Well, Majorca to be precise.'

'Right.' Cullen made a note. 'Whereabouts?'

'Shagaluf.' Tommy sniffed. 'Actually stayed in a hotel on that street a few years back. Boys' weekend. Cracking fun.'

'You got the history?'

'You got the warrant?'

'Come on, Tommy...'

'For the history, I really do need the paperwork before I start, so please.'

'Will do.' But it looked like a dead end. Would've been a good suspect, but it was just way too neat.

Cullen looked around the place. Not far from Anderson and his SOCO mob. Bit too quiet for his liking. 'Where is everyone?'

'Off out for lunch. Boss's orders.'

'Anderson?'

'One and the bloody same. All one happy family now. Told us to get away from our desks when we're eating. Lost a couple of phones to Wee Doug spilling Dr Pepper over them. Wouldn't hear that it's Wee Doug who's the problem, not the rest of us.'

'Anderson about?'

'Not sure. I try to keep a mile away from the prat.'

Cullen got up with a smile. 'Give me a call if that phone moves.'

'Who is it, like?'

'A suspect. Need to know if she was anywhere near Ashworth's in Gilmerton last night.'

'And you know you need to fill out paperwork even for what we've just done.'

'Come on, Tommy.'

'Listen, Scott. You're a DI now. Never thought I'd see the day, but you've got to cut out all that malarkey, okay? Do the job properly.'

'Fine. I'll get it to you by close of play.'

'Good man.' Tommy reached into his bag for a metal sandwich box. He winked and put a finger to his lips.

Cullen walked off, shaking his head for effect, and opened the door to the forensics lab. He had to search round five corners in a room that should only have four, but there was no sign of James Anderson.

Maybe he was making sure his new policy was enforced across all his staff. And no wonder they were taking so long with everything if they lost an hour of people working through lunch every day.

Cullen got out his mobile and called Deeley.

'Ah, young Skywalker. How goes it?'

'Not great. Don't know if you've heard, but I've got a dead body who needs a post-mortem.'

'Oh yes, of course I heard. And I'm still hamstrung by the lack of forensics.'

'I don't see how.'

'Scott, I examine bodies in situ, then I examine them here, more thoroughly. To give a full and accurate assessment, the in situ part—i.e. the crime scene—is as crucial as weighing the victim's innards and listening to DS Bain joking about his todger.'

'So you need James Anderson's report?'

'Correctamundo. Blood toxicology will get me most of the way there.'

Cullen found a sixth corner to look around, but still no sign of anybody, so he headed back over to Anderson's desk and sat on the edge. 'Well, I'm in the lab and nobody's around.'

'Typical. I warned the powers that be that this would happen.'

'That what would happen?'

'You're not the only ambitious scamp around here, Scott. When you lot moved from Leith Walk to St Leonards, they merged IT Forensics and Telephony under Crime Scene Management. Across Police Scotland, it saved them six high-paying admin jobs. Trouble is, he's in charge of the East division and is making a royal mess of everything.'

'Tommy Smith told me this already.'

'Well, I'm telling you now. Anderson's drowning. He might be half-decent at finding a used rubber in a crime scene, but see managing clowns like Charlie Kidd and Tommy Smith? Forget it. Bane of my life.'

'Well. My bane is called Brian Bain.'

'But for how much longer?'

'What's that supposed to mean?'

'It's not just forensics I'm asked to consult on. Anyhoo, I've got to go. Tatty bye!'

'Jimmy, wait!' But he was gone.

Cullen sighed and slumped into Anderson's chair. Very comfortable, much better than what he had upstairs.

He knew part of what Deeley was rabbiting on about, though. Those precious "efficiencies" that were pretty much all Police Scotland stood for. Merging everything made sense until it was just one cop doing all the work and there was bedlam on the streets.

But Bain not being a problem any more? Did that mean he'd be gone soon? Or would Cullen?

'See if you've changed any of the settings, I swear.' Anderson dumped his metal piece box on the table in front of Cullen. 'Shift.'

Cullen didn't move. 'So long as you fast track the work for the PM.'

'Come on, you twat. My back's buggered from all the crouching and kneeling at crime scenes. That chair's bloody expensive.'

'Fine, but please, you need to fast-track the blood toxicology.'

'I keep telling you—'

'I'm running out of leads here, and you're my only hope, Obi-Wan.'

'You've been speaking to Deeley, haven't you? I swear...'

'Just please try and fast-track it.'

'Like I keep telling you and him, we've got a ton of active murders to process, so things are going to take time.'

'It's just a case of doing that one bit of analysis, then I'll be out of your hair.'

That seemed to tempt him a bit. 'No, Scott, it's never that. With you and with Deeley, it's always a ton of shite dropped over my head. And Tommy Smith says you're at it again. Tracing phone numbers without a RIPSA? Come on.'

'I told him I'd get the form to him by close of day.'

'Cool. He'll start work on it tomorrow, then.'

'Come on, mate.'

Anderson laughed. 'Don't you mate me. After all the shite you've been—' He collapsed into his chair and screamed. 'Ah, you fucker!'

'What's up?'

'You've fucked about with my settings!' Anderson jerked upright, both hands on his lumbar region. 'For crying out loud, this will set me right back. You just come in here and think you can mess around with stuff? Scott, this is me crippled for a month now!'

'I've no idea what's happened. I haven't so much as breathed on your seat.'

Anderson couldn't bring himself to look at Cullen. He just stood there, kneading at his lower back. Frowning. Then scowling. 'Where is it?'

'Where's what.'

Anderson jerked forward and tore open the door to a desktop fridge. The thing was humming loud now. 'The beef.'

'What beef?'

'What we found in the fucking victim's fucking mouth! It's gone!'

15

BAIN

The wee interview room stinks of rusty metal and bleach, way worse than it usually does. And it's all coming from this fud.

Keith Ross, conspiracy nut, supermarket cleaner. Big sweaty bastard. I tell you, I expected him to crumble in seconds in an interview room with the heater turned up—kaboom, all you want to know—but no, he's keeping fuckin' quiet, and he hasn't even got a brief in with him. 'I have no idea what you're on about.' The boy is super-stoned, can't imagine he knows which solar system he's in, let alone which planet he's on. 'Is that guy going to be okay?'

'Which guy?'

He points at the big plaster on his forehead. 'The one who smacked into me. He was losing a lot of blood.'

'He's at the dental hospital, son. Sure they'll fix it.'

'Okay.'

'Son, your work key's missing. A colleague's killed and you're saying you've no idea who'd take it?'

'I'm a wanted man.'

Elvis laughs at that, but catches my look. 'This isn't funny, sir.'

Fuck it, here we go. I lean across the table and let this big sack of armpit sweat taste my digesting lunch. 'What are you up to?'

'Nothing.'

'Son, who did you give your key to?'

'No idea.'

'Wait, so you gave it to someone and you've no idea who they are?'

'No! I didn't give it to anyone!'

'Sure about that?'

'Are you working for *them*?'

I glance at Elvis and the boy looks as puzzled as yours truly. 'Who's them?'

'The CIA? MI6? Mossad? Take your pick. They're all after me.'

Forget the chemtrails in the sky and on his T-shirt, the chemicals in here have clearly warped the boy's mind.

'What about FSB?'

'The Russians...' The cleaner shakes his head. 'You know, they get a bad press but they're not the worst.'

Fuck this for a game of soldiers. 'Enough of the conspiracy shite, son. A young lad with his life ahead of him was killed in that supermarket. That's real, okay? No conspiracy, no bullshit, just a tragic event. You're getting the chance to help us here.'

He purses his lips like that bird in that show back in the Nineties. What a wanker.

I thumb at Elvis. 'Want me to call up my wee pal in MI6?'

'I don't leave a trace.'

'No, you do. Everyone does. They'll have a file on you.'

The boy raises his hands, up high. 'You can't arrest me for searching for the truth!'

I get out my phone, then shove that photo of the supermarket vulture at him. 'You know this guy, right?'

'No.'

'Come on, enough of that. This guy was seen in an altercation with Philip Turnbull last night. Next thing we know, he's dead. We have it on good authority that you know him. So. Out with it.'

'Aye, I know him a bit. Chat to him about truth.'

'Truth, right.'

'His name's Derek Keeley, but everyone calls him Del. He's big on the secret space program, particularly the Nazis.'

'The *what?*'

Elvis pipes up. 'They had flying saucers, Sarge.'

How deep does this shite go with these arseholes?

I mean, if you listen to Sundance or Crystal, they'd think I was the bonkers one, but Christ on the cross, people actually believe this shite?

But I don't let my glare drift away from Keith fuckin' Ross. 'You know where he lives?'

'No.'

'He ever share any of this Nazi space program nonsense with you?'

'It's not nonsense. I've got—'

'Do you have his phone number or email address?'

'Right.' The big bastard glances up at the clock. 'I know him online. He's done some YouTube stuff, comments on a lot of my videos.'

'You got a username for him?'

'I'd have to check.' He's gesturing to Elvis with freaky little hands. Never noticed before how small they are. 'On my phone.'

'Not so fast.'

He sighs. 'Right.'

'Know anything else about him?'

'From the chats we've had in the shop, I think he's a translator, German to English, English to German, can't remember which. Works from home, but he likes to get the bargains. Asks me to keep an eye on the good stuff, so I've helped him a few times.' He looks up at the clock. 'He'll be heading to Asda just now.'

'Why?'

'They reduce their prices round about now. Sainsbury's on the hour, Tesco only twice a day.'

16

CULLEN

'Because you sodding lost evidence!' Eyes shut, Methven kicked his office chair back and stood to jab his finger at Anderson. 'How do you explain it?'

'Well it was there before lunch. I came back and it was gone.' Anderson nodded at Cullen. 'He was there, though.'

Methven trained his fire at Cullen. 'What were you doing?'

Cullen took a deep breath, trying to divert the worst of his thoughts before he said too much that he regretted. 'I was looking for him. Deeley needs the blood toxicology to finish the PM.'

Methven stared hard at Cullen. 'Did you take the meat?'

'Seriously? Of course I didn't.'

'Colin, he was right—'

'Enough!' Methven powered over to the door and yanked it open. 'Get the hell out of here and find it!'

'Sure.' Anderson sloped off.

Through the door, Cullen spotted a few faces looking his way. People in his team, people in the other two. All very interested in who was getting their arse handed to them. He shut the door and leaned back against it, facing Methven. 'I'm sorry, sir.'

Methven took a seat. 'You're *sorry*?'

Cullen left the safety of the door and walked over to the seat nearest his desk. 'Sir, I—'

'Don't sit down!'

'Right, sir.'

'Why the sodding hell are you sorry?'

'Because our case is buggered, isn't it? It was in the victim's mouth and Anderson was testing it for poison. If Deeley finds that he was poisoned, we need that to prove that's how the poison got into his system. Given where we are on this case, with a million and one suspects, we really need to close down the cause of death.'

'Okay...' Methven sat back in his chair, eyes shut, the lids flickering. He opened them again, staring hard at Cullen. 'Did you steal the meat?'

'First, I already told you, no. Second, no. Third, why the hell would I? Fourth, no. Fifth, where would I have put it? Sixth, no. Seventh, can't believe you think I would. Eighth, I can't believe you'd ask me twice.'

'I trusted you to run this case while I dealt with a pressing strategic matter.' Methven stood up tall. 'Scott, James Anderson is for the high jump here. He left that evidence in a fridge in an unlocked office while his staff were all at lunch. Whether you took it or not, you need to find that sodding meat.'

17

BAIN

Chesser Asda is the best supermarket in the UK, I swear.

We're in the booze aisle, me and Elvis, just two boys checking out craft beer. Got a good view across the aisle to the bread and meat counters, both still quiet and tranquil.

I spot a good deal on that nice gin the other half enjoys. Should really pick up a bottle, but Elvis will probably grass. I mean, he probably won't, but can't take the chance with Crystal and Sundance both having me in their sights. 'For once, Elvis my boy, we could use that podcast as a real cover story. The look on Cunter's face when we catch this boy.'

'Cunter?'

'It's my new name for him.'

'Not really one of your best, is it?' Elvis puts his phone away with a snide grin. 'Cullen was asking me about all your swearing, so I'd look for something else. Like Munter.'

'What the fuck's a munter?'

'An ugly bastard.'

'Aye, that works.'

'Anyhoo, I got a text from Buxton.'

'Aye?'

'They've saved both teeth.'

'Shame.'

'Come on, that's a bit harsh. He was just doing his job.'

'He made an arse of it. Tough justice.'

'The cleaner opened his door. That's hardly—'

'Shhh.'

The boy with the pricing gun is pushing his trolley towards the reductions aisle.

'Look around, and spot a ton of vultures waiting to pounce.'

'You're a bit of a vulture, aren't you, Bri?'

I give him that look, but he doesn't shut up.

'Seen you in the Tesco on Leith Walk a few times, waiting to pounce on the sandwiches at half three. This is before I knew you, like.'

Sneaky bastard. 'Those were the glory days before the minimum pricing on booze came in. Tell you, I got a great deal on an IPA once. Actually, we had it during our first podcast.'

'Aye?'

'Think it was called "Same Room as a Monster" or something. Stopped making it. Lush, wasn't it?'

There's movement from the vultures, though, as the boy with the gun sticks a whole free-range chicken on the shelf in the fridge. Had a look at it earlier and was moderately tempted at three quid, but he's taken it down another peg. Two quid and I'd snap his arm off. All the vultures start wandering over, closing in on it.

But someone swoops in from the milk aisle and fuck me if it's not Del Keeley. He snatches it off the shelf and pops it in his basket, then fucks off quicksmart. What a boy.

'Sir!' Elvis is loping ahead of us, but running isn't his best attribute, put it that way, so he's at a quick walk. 'Police!'

The boy glances round, but he's already dropped his basket, so he just fuckin' wanders off, hands up. Nothing to see here, officer.

Fuck sake.

I tear off after them, trying not to disturb anyone. Elvis is closing in on the outside, mincing away like one of those boys in the Olympic walking. Heading deep into the store, likes. Aha, the boy takes a left towards the freezers.

Here's where I excel. Like a fuckin' chess player me, seven or eight moves ahead. I duck down the milk aisle and weave between two auld wifies talking shite, then break into a jog and pop out at the bottom by the fresh pizzas. Back up the aisle, Elvis is chatting to the lad.

Bollocks.

Well, my move would've paid off if he hadn't caught up with him. So, I take it slow, in case he runs. Can't be arsed with a run, like, not these days. Sundance is always at it, but fuck that.

And, SHITE, the boy clocks us and his eyes go wide. He pushes Elvis, sending him arse over tit into an open freezer thing. Bags of peas spill out and green ball bearings scatter over the floor.

I'm running after the boy, but the gap is fuckin' widening with each stride I take.

A bag of peas flies through the air and clonks the boy on the head. Bingo, he's down on the floor.

Simple task for me to snap the cuffs on the lad. 'Let's have a wee word down the station, shall we? Assaulting a police officer is a very serious offence.'

∽

I'M in the longer corridor in St Leonards. Fuck sake. No idea why they built it that way, but it does my head in. Feels like it runs through to Glasgow it's that fuckin' long.

And I'm fuckin' starving.

The door opens and Elvis steps out with a wide grin on his face. 'No lawyer.'

'He doesn't want one?'

He shakes his head. 'And I got it on tape.'

'Right, here we go.' I crack my knuckles, then put a hand on the door handle, ready to execute one of my well-known pincer movements on a prime suspect. Get right in their face before they even notice the door opening.

'Sarge.' Hunter's powering towards us, face like a slapped arse too. 'Got a problem.'

Those three little words…

I let go of the handle. 'Go on.'

'I can't make head nor tail of the data.' Prick's got a laptop under his oxter.

'Craig, you've got one job here. If you can't handle spread-sheets, you should've stayed in the Sexual Offences unit.' Boy looks like a sex offender, that's for sure. Might've used that gag on Sundance's ex, though. Shite. Fuck it, change tack. 'I gather it wasn't your choice to move here, was it?'

Hunter lets out a deep sigh and it's like he's counting to ten.

'Is this you telling me you can't do the job and I need to give it to DC Gordon?'

Elvis is giving me pure evils, I tell you.

'Pretty much.' Hunter stares right at us and fuck me does he needs a better nickname than Cunter. 'I'm good at some things, not so good at others. I'm man enough to admit it.'

'Right.' Fuck sake. This sort of shite always blows back on us, despite everything I fuckin' do to help these useless bastards. 'Go get it all set up, then DC Gordon will come and help you.'

'Thanks.'

'And stop being such a useless cunt.'

'What did you say?'

'You heard.'

He drops the laptop to the floor and gets right in my face. 'You fucking little worm. I'll crush you and—'

'Get off him, Craig!' Elvis, the voice of reason for once, managing to haul him away. 'I'll come find you in a bit, all right?'

'No. Elvis, you fuckin' do it. Craig, make yourself useful by getting me a fuckin' coffee. I'll get Caldwell in here to sort this shite out.' I slip inside the room like a shadow, not a bull in a china shop.

18

CULLEN

Cullen wandered through the station, his head fizzing. Two colleagues stopped to let him through the fire door first, but he pushed into the locker room. The place was empty, pretty much the only thing good about it. He collapsed onto the bench in front of his own locker.

And he just couldn't work out what was going on. He couldn't even remember seeing the fridge when he entered the lab, let alone the meat inside it. Usually he'd hear the humming, and it was loud, but nothing.

How the hell could it have gone missing? Was the killer someone on the inside? Or was someone working with the killer?

Neither option filled him with anything other than revulsion.

The alternative was someone messing with him. Anderson,

maybe. Hard to pin anything down to him, just constant aggro between them.

Whatever. He couldn't do anything about it.

Yeah, right. Like he'd ever just given up on anything like this.

He slumped back and thumped his head against the locker door.

Time was, he'd have fought it, probably even have fought Methven, or at least offered to go outside. At least he would've told Methven exactly what he thought of him and the accusations.

But now... Now he needed to act like a DI, even if he was only Acting DI. Yeah, ridiculous though it was, he had to act like an Acting DI.

And he could see it from Methven's point of view as a DCI. All he had was Cullen in a room he shouldn't have been in, and some key evidence going missing. As much as he hated it, Cullen could empathise with Crystal Methven.

A crash came from the toilets.

What the hell?

Cullen got up and walked through, taking it very slowly. Last time he'd heard anything like this was that old guy having a heart attack in a stationery cupboard.

The first door hung open and a pair of boots poked out into the bathroom.

Cullen recognised them. Big chunky Timberlands, a fashion salved from the early 2000s. 'Craig?'

No response.

Cullen sneaked forward a few more steps and peered in.

Hunter was sitting on the pan, staring into space. Trousers up, thankfully, but his lips were moving in fast twitches, his eyes joining in every few seconds.

Cullen didn't know what to do. Was he hallucinating? Was he sleepwalking? Having a fit?

Sod it.

He grabbed his arm. 'Craig!'

Hunter jerked upright and stepped into a fighting stance, pushing Cullen back against the opposite stall door. He stood there, breathing hard and fast, his face screwed tight, but his eyes were somewhere else. Probably back in Iraq. Then something softened in him, and he shut his eyes. 'Scott?'

'You okay?'

Hunter swallowed hard. 'It's my PTSD.'

'Thought you were over that.'

'Me too. These drugs aren't obviously designed for dealing with Bain.'

'What's he done?'

'Just his usual. I almost lamped him.'

'I've almost lamped him a few times. That's also known as letting him win.' Cullen tried a smile, but Hunter didn't join it. 'Anything I can do to help?'

'Sack him? Give me to another DS?'

'You know I can't let Chantal manage you, but I'll see what I can do.' Cullen pointed through to the locker room. 'Let's get out of the toilet. People will talk about us.'

Finally, Hunter smiled. 'Aren't they talking already?' And he set off through the toilet back into the locker room, perching opposite Cullen's locker.

'You want to tell me exactly what happened?'

'Right. So Bain's got me getting hold of the Ashworth's customer data and processing it, trying to find some guy who might've got into a fight with the victim.'

'A fight?'

'Heated argument, maybe.' Hunter nibbled at a fingernail. 'All that data stuff isn't exactly my strength.'

'You need a hand?'

'I'll be fine.'

'Sure? I can get Elvis on it.'

'I said I'm fine. How hard can it be if Elvis can do it?'

Cullen shrugged. He looked for his locker key, but it wasn't in his pocket, so he had to find the one on his keyring, hidden among the seeming hundreds of keys he'd acquired, then put it in the lock. 'Elvis can do it in five minutes, maybe less, and you can show him how to do the stuff you're good at.'

'Bain's had him doing that. It's not going well. You should have a word with him.'

'Would that I could. So do you want me to—'

'That's the problem, Scott. Bain's passed it on to him already.'

'Right.'

'What's going on, anyway? Why are you in here?'

Cullen looked over. 'I'm...' He didn't have the words.

'Stropping? What about?'

'Some evidence went walkabouts.' Saying it out loud gave Cullen a flash of pure rage, right down in the pit of his stomach. 'Anderson's fucked up royally, but Methven isn't impressed with me.'

'What?' Hunter sat next to him. 'Why?'

'Exactly. It doesn't make any sense to me.'

'Has someone stolen it?'

'We don't know.'

'Right, so this I can help with. Let me find out who's taken it.'

'You're assuming it was taken.'

'What do you mean?'

'Hanlon's razor. "Never attribute to malice that which is adequately explained by stupidity". Anderson's taken on another two departments and is burning the candle at both ends, fucking everything up, left right and centre. He's lost it, pure and simple, and he's blaming me.'

'Aye, and that's—'

The door opened and Methven stormed in. He didn't say

anything, just stood there, hand in his pocket, jangling his keys like there was no tomorrow.

Cullen hauled himself up to standing. 'Sir, I think you need to—'

'Shut up.' Methven jabbed a finger at Cullen. 'This is unacceptable.'

Cullen turned back round to face his locker. Only way he could think to block him out. And getting his stuff and clearing off would be the best move.

'Look at me when I'm talking to you.'

Cullen didn't. He twisted the locker key. 'Sir, this is complete bullshit. Why would I steal that meat?'

'Because you're working with the killer?'

'Listen to yourself.' Cullen gritted his teeth, still facing away from the colossal prick. 'Have you got any evidence of that?'

Methven didn't have a reply. His jangling of keys was the only sound in there.

Cullen took one look at Hunter, got a flash of eyebrows, then opened his locker, desperate to get out of there.

A sealed evidence bag sat on top of his trainers. The meat!

'Holy shit.' Hunter was staring at it. 'Is that—'

Methven elbowed him aside. 'Neither of you move!' He snapped on a pair of gloves and pulled the bag out. 'You just found it.'

Cullen stepped away from him. 'I swear it was just sitting there.'

'Are you two cooking this up?' Methven shut his eyes. 'Pardon the sodding pun.'

'No, sir, we're not.' Cullen waited for him to open his eyes again, then fixed him with the hardest stare he could muster without throwing a fist at him. 'Sir, I couldn't find my locker key and—'

'You lost it?'

'I keep my spare on my keyring and—'

'This is ridiculous, the pair of you are—'

Cullen looked at Hunter, leading with him. 'Craig, tell him?'

'I saw what I saw, sir. Scott was talking and he found it.'

Methven shook his head. 'Whoever stole this is probably working with our killer.'

Cullen wasn't sure he bought it. 'Maybe. But they're trying to frame me.'

'Okay, so assuming this isn't you and Craig trying to dig you out of a very deep hole...'

'If you're giving us a chance to confess, there's nothing to confess to, sir.'

'I see. If I find that you've taken it, then—'

'You won't find that, because I haven't.'

'If I do, then I'll have to suspend you.' Methven glowered at him. 'But right now, you're going to take it back and we'll deal with how it got there later.' He held up the bag. 'Given the meat is still in this, the chain of custody is maintained. We need to get this checked.'

19

BAIN

I'm being the big man here and letting her take charge.

DC Angela Caldwell. Giant of a lassie, a good six, seven inches taller than yours truly. Fuckin' stunner too, despite having two kids. Bet Sundance has tried it on with her, what with her being a recent widow and all that. She slides a CCTV still over the desk, calm as you like, taking it nice and slow. Professional. Way better than Hunter or Elvis.

The boy's beak is *giant*, I tell you. Like a fuckin' budgie, he could open seeds with that hooter. Not that the real Budgie will be picking anything up with his teeth for a while. Actually feel a bit sorry for the poor bastard. Anyway, it's hard to pick out anything else in this boy, he's just so fuckin' normal looking except for that conk. He takes one look at the photo, then grasps his nose like it's a kid's teddy bear or comfort blanket. 'Right.'

'Right?'

'Aye, right.'

'Care to explain this, sir?'

'Not really.'

'This is you, right?'

'Hard to disagree with that, aye.'

'For the benefit of the tape, the suspect is referencing photograph catalogued as P-07. You know this man?'

'Had a few run-ins, aye.'

'What about?'

The boy grins. 'The price of bread in southern Edinburgh.'

'Go on.' She's good, this one. Cold as ice.

'Right, that boy was goading me.'

'How?'

'See, they've got all this bread coming in every day. Loaves and loaves of the stuff and at massively inflated prices. How much does it cost to make a loaf? Flour, salt, yeast, water. And they're charging a pound for a loaf. A *pound*.' Boy's snarling like he's been charged a grand for a late library book. 'How can they justify that?'

'We live in a market economy and it's what people are prepared to pay.'

'Aye, well, it's bullshit.' Del Keeley stabs a finger at the page. 'This boy wasn't reducing the bread enough.'

'What's enough?'

'10p absolute max, obviously.'

'It's not obvious to me.'

'Suit yourself.'

'So how much was he pricing it at?'

'20p. That's *outrageous* for a loaf of bread.'

She taps the page again. 'Seem to be a lot of people taking up that offer.'

'Well, they're idiots.'

'I don't get the problem.'

'Listen, I've got four kids and they go through bread like

nobody's business. Plus all this shite in China? I've got a freezer full of bread at home and an attic full of bog paper. You wait, I'm well prepared for the apocalypse. But I'm not going to pay these extortionate rates for a loaf of bread.'

'You could make it yourself?'

'Have you seen what they're charging for flour?'

'How much do you spend on fuel to travel between these shops?'

'That's beside the point.'

'Sure about that?'

'Well, they're all around Isla's nursery and James's school, so it's not exactly out of my way.' He snarls. 'And I've got a sourdough on the go, but the kids don't like it, do they? Thanks to their grandmother, all they'll eat is white bread. *With the crusts off!* Absolute living hell, I tell you.'

Had enough of this bozo, so I lean over and whisper to Caldwell, 'This guy is just an idiot taking the mick.'

She nods back, but doesn't say anything, at least not to me. 'Where were you last night?'

'After the supermarket, I collected the kids from afterschool. Then did the usual at home, all night.'

'And this morning?'

'Getting the kids ready for school. An absolute bloody nightmare. Then dropping them off and of course that snooty cow who always seems to think it's weird that a man drops his kids off, she went off on one at me about her kids not getting vaccinated and how mine were endangering hers. I mean—'

'Aside from this fellow parent, can anyone account for your whereabouts?'

'Well, the wife got back in about nine, and she was off at the crack of sparrow fart this morning.'

'Oh?'

'She's a lawyer. Working really long hours just now. The world's going crazy.'

She's looking at Del Keeley and tapping the page again. 'Do you know this man?'

'I told you, he keeps on refusing to reduce the bread to an acceptable level.'

'Do you know his name?'

'No!'

Christ, she's dangerously competent. So I grab the boy's attention. 'You were obviously very angry with him, one might say enraged, murderous. Bet you would have liked to be alone with him for a bit with that price gun of his, eh? Did you go there first thing and kill him?'

'Of course not! I've not got the time to have a dump without a kid bursting in, let alone concoct a scheme to murder someone.'

He frowns at the page, then prods the paper. 'I know *him*, though. Simon Mowat.'

I snatch up the page. It's the boy who was mis-pricing a steak. 'How do you know him?'

'Sit a few seats down from him at Tynecastle, and I always see him in the shops around this time. Another yellow item fiend.'

'Thank you, sir.' I give Caldwell the thumbs up. 'Let him go, aye?'

She leans over to kill the interview as I'm striding out of the room. Cock on! Good old Brian Bain with a lead. This'll show fuckin' Sundance a thing or two.

Elvis is lurking in the room opposite, tapping at a keyboard but with a face like a slapped arse. With piles. That hasn't wiped properly.

'You okay there, Paul?'

He looks up at us. 'I'm going through the data Hunter got and I'll be buggered if I can make head nor tail of any of it.'

'Try searching for a Simon Mowat.'

'How are you spelling that?'

'S-I-M-O-N.' Fuckin' twat.

'I know that. The surname.'

'M-O-W-A-T.'

'Nope.'

'What do you mean, nope?'

'Can't find it.' He frowns. 'I've got a Simon MOET, like the champagne?'

20

CULLEN

Cullen stayed as far from the body as he could manage, trying to avoid looking at Deeley slicing into flesh.

'Young Skywalker, I can only apologise for how much of a step down my new lair is from my old one.'

Cullen looked around the ancient room with its vaulted brick ceilings, masked by modern concrete and glass. 'It's fine.'

'Back to the Cowgate and its ageing mortuary, a world away from the high-tech modernity we used to enjoy.' Something thumped against metal. 'Police Scotland's budget couldn't support our brave new world. The one who suffered most from you all decamping back to St Leonards was me. I'm just collateral damage.'

'You've kept your machines and stuff, though.'

'When the power's up and running. It's sporadic. Through in Glasgow, they have a world-class facility in Govan.'

'I've seen it.'

'Oh, yes, I forgot.' Another thud. 'Well, well, well.'

Cullen finally looked over.

Anderson was standing by the door, smoothing down his goatee. 'You get that file, Jim?'

'Sure thing.' Deeley beamed at him, then picked up a tablet computer. 'Aha.' He looked over at Anderson with an arched eyebrow. 'Sure?'

'I think so. I just do my bit, you're responsible for the rest of it.'

Cullen finally took in the body, the pale flesh sliced wide open. Blank eyes, wide-open mouth. 'You want to tell me what's going on?'

'Well, young Skywalker, your friend and mine, James Anderson... Surely he's not your favourite of the many Jameses in your orbit?'

'Not even top three.'

Anderson shook his head, a wry grin on his face.

Deeley caressed the cadaver's cheek like it was a lover. 'Okay, well, the poisoned meat didn't kill him. It was the suffocation.'

'Sure?'

'As sure as I can be.' Deeley winced. 'Whoever did this knocked him out first.' He tapped the victim's skull. 'A blow here, peri-mortem. Blunt-force trauma, so I'd say a baseball bat or a crowbar.'

'So they might be a reluctant killer?'

'Good question, young Skywalker. It might just be someone who didn't like risks. But that's your job to figure out, not mine.'

'Still don't get why they'd stuff meat into his mouth.'

Deeley ran a finger across the victim's bottom lip. 'The stickers would've secured his mouth and prevented a gag reaction. All the killer would need to do is hold his nose and wait.'

Cullen tried to process it all. Deeley's take certainly made sense. The shadowy figure on the CCTV coupled with the blow to the head showed a likelier timeline. 'How long was he lying there?'

'Not long. Mr Anderson here has managed to confirm that the heating in that place had only been at full blast since quarter to six, not all night. And I'd say that's your time of death.' Deeley touched the victim's top lip and brushed something away. 'Mr Turnbull's death was quick. Less than a minute, I'd say.'

Still a horrible way to go. 'Right. Better go and brief the boss.'

THE COWGATE THRUMMED WITH LIFE, the commuter rush hour kicking in early tonight, cars and lorries all jockeying for position.

Cullen got behind the wheel and started the car. Going to be a while before he could get out into that.

'Well.' Sounded like Methven was in his office, shouting into his headset, as per usual these days. 'Well, it's a preliminary finding, but we should progress on that basis now. Do you have a suspect in mind?'

'The supermarket was involved in a poisoned meat scandal three years previously where five people died. Add in that Philip Turnbull's father is the local butcher and my alarm bells are ringing loud.'

Silence at the other end of the line.

Cullen pulled off into the slow-moving traffic, heading for the Pleasance and the climb out of the pit of the Cowgate and towards Gilmerton. 'Sir?'

'You think he killed his own son?'

'No, sir. Not yet anyway. But three people died and he clearly profited from it. Hard not to think someone's got a motive to target his son. Maybe even him.'

21

BAIN

Elvis is behind the wheel and the car's getting cold already. He points upstairs. 'The lad lives up there.'

'Cool.' I look around the area, just as the street-lights switch on. Bit of a shite street, this. As much as they cleaned up Niddrie, it's still a fuckin' cesspit. Lots of posh cars, mind. What does that tell you? 'Whichever fanny put his record as MOET needs a fuckin' kick up the hoop.'

'I'll hold them down while you kick away, Bri.'

A battered old Nissan pulls up opposite us, and Caldwell gets out in instalments. Christ, but she really is tall.

I open my door but don't get out. 'You stay in the car.'

'Come on, Sarge.'

'I'm not joking around here, Paul.' Use his Christian name, show I mean business. 'If this boy is behind this, chances are he'll foxtrot oscar, sharpish. I want you in this bad boy, ready to chase him down.'

'Right.'

Christ, it's like dealing with a child all over again. 'Come on, if I knew where the hell Hunter was, I'd give him this donkey work. He's actually good at chases, but I need you on this. I can trust you.'

He sniffs. 'Cheers.'

I open the door wide and it's Baltic out there. 'Keep your phone on, aye?'

He tugs at the charging cable. 'Ready and willing.'

'Good lad.' I nudge the door shut and make my way across the road.

Caldwell's scanning the houses. 'Upstairs, right?'

'So Elvis says.'

The house is split up like a Battenberg cake, four sections of horror. Lights on in three, bottom left looks empty. Actually, wonder if Ashworth's are selling off any Battenbergs?

FOCUS.

'Right, Batgirl. You lead.'

'Sure.' She opens the gate and it squeals like someone's stepped on its ballsack. Four buzzers by the door, though. 'Mowat, right?'

'Right.'

She hits one and leans in.

'Aye?' Male voice, nasal and distorted.

'Police, sir.'

'What?'

'Police.'

'Cannae hear you.' And he's gone.

'What is wrong with people?' She's hammering the button again. 'It's always been like this, hasn't it?'

'Nah. In all my days on the force, these are the darkest, that's for sure.'

She hits the button again and holds it down. 'Should we—?'

The door clatters open and a hand lashes out, knocking Caldwell's finger off the button. 'Quit it! My mother's asleep!'

It's the boy from the supermarket, alright. Simon Mowat. The cheeky bastard is getting in her face, but he's wearing a pinny, all flowers and butterflies. Hope for his sake it's ironic. He balls up a fist and takes a backswing.

Caldwell might be tall as fuck but she's *fast*. She grabs his wrist and twists. The boy's on his knees before I can think of anything funny to say.

'Let go of us!'

'Are you going to calm down?'

'Aye, aye.'

She looks at me, eyebrows raised, and I nod, so she lets go.

The boy gets back up, rubbing at his wrists. 'What's going on?'

Caldwell waves her warrant card in his face. 'Police.'

'What?'

'Need you to come with us to the station, sir.'

'I can't.'

'Aye, you can.' My turn to take over, throw a bit of seniority around here. 'And you are.'

'Are what?'

'Coming down the station!'

'But my mum isn't well! She needs her drugs!'

A voice comes from upstairs, harsh and shrill. 'Simon, how much longer are my eggs going to be?'

The boy rolls his eyes at us. 'I've got three poaching just now.'

Time for some fuckin' excellent leadership here. 'DC Caldwell, I need you to stay and look after her, okay?'

Sounds like she mutters, 'Fuck sake.'

22

Cullen

Ashworth's car park was still empty, with just one bank of lights on inside. No other signs of life and that was probably a security measure.

Cullen rapped on the glass again, though, but it didn't look like anyone was in there, let alone anyone who could answer the door.

A trail of lights winked on, heading towards them. A lumbering figure appeared around the tills. The cleaner, stomping heavily. The door opened and he peered out. 'Guys, I'm under pressure here. Just got the go-ahead to open tomorrow and the boss has me doing a deep clean. And I had to get interviewed again, so I'll be here all night thanks to DI Bain.'

Bain using his previous rank to bully someone. Great.

'Well, that's news to me.' Cullen checked his phone and had a missed call from Methven and an accompanying text.

Ashw open tomorrow. Please call me

Nothing from Bain, though. Sneaky bugger was hiding something.

Cullen focused on the cleaner again. 'Thanks for agreeing to interview. It might help us solve this case.'

'Won't help me clean this place, though. My boss is going apeshit.'

Hunter stepped forward. 'You find your key yet?'

'Nope. Weird as hell. I think a ghost took it, mind.'

'A *ghost*?'

'Aye. My flat's haunted. This old wifie, occasionally see her. She moves stuff around. She must've taken it.'

Hunter shook his head. 'Is Adam Searle here?'

'Aye, just in his office on the phone to management. Want me to show you through?'

'Please.' Hunter let Cullen go first.

Cullen kept pace with the cleaner, but it was slow going. 'You work here during that meat poisoning scandal?'

'Shitest business, aye. Kept thinking this place was going to shut. Had to get in a load of investment, way I hear it.' The cleaner tapped his nose. 'Saudi money.'

Cullen caught Hunter's smirk. 'Right.'

'My theory is it was Mossad behind it, but it could be the CIA, at a push.'

'Anyone lose their job?'

'Well, Adam almost did. He was the butcher, wasn't he? Kept getting fingered for it, but they think it was an outside job.'

'Who do?'

'Management. Brought in a private eye to look into it.'

'Not the police?'

'Oh aye, couldn't move for you lot sniffing around, but I think that was you lot just installing security measures to monitor me. The way Adam explained it, though, management just wanted assurance that it wasn't anything really snide.

Sometimes people don't want to talk to feds, but they'll talk to a PI.'

Seemed strange to Cullen, but then he'd seen his share of corporate tricks and bullshit. 'But Mr Searle kept his job?'

'Got promoted, if you ask me.' Ross sniffed. 'Course, it was kind of compensation.'

'What for?'

'Well, Adam lost his daughter to some poisoned meat.'

Cullen stopped, just metres from the door to the back of the shop. 'You're serious?'

'Aye. Adam and his missus were both ill, but they pulled through. Their kid was in the hospital and died. And now his wife won't even speak to him.'

Cullen charged off through the door into the back room, then darted up the steps. The staff canteen was dead, but a light haloed the office door. Cullen tore it open.

Adam Searle was sitting behind the desk, feet up, on the phone. 'Well, he's going to see if he can. It's been hell.' He squinted round at them. 'Gotta go.' He jerked upright. 'What's up?'

Cullen walked up to the desk and stood far enough away to be irritating. 'You didn't think to tell us about your daughter?'

'Shite.' Searle collapsed back against his desk, knocking the phone onto the floor. 'Shite.'

'A man's dead and you didn't think to say that you had a motive?'

'Shite.'

'Where is your ex-wife?'

'What?' Searle sniffed. 'Haven't heard from Jen for months until the divorce hearing last night. Said she had a bit of bother at work and was off on holiday.'

'Where does she work?'

'The university.'

'Jen?' Cullen shut his eyes. No, no, no, no. 'Is her name Jenny Black?'

'Maiden name, aye. Why?'

'That bother at work? She was sleeping with a student. Stole an exam paper. The student was Philip Turnbull.'

'Oh my god.' Searle covered his mouth with his hand. 'My effing therapist says I should be more sympathetic, about how we both went through the same thing. It's just really hard when she cuts you out of her life and blames you for everything that happened. Jen always blamed Phil's dad for the tainted meat, reckoned he planted it in the shop.'

TURNBULL'S WAS SHUT. No lights on inside, even in the faint twilight.

Hunter peered though the glass. 'Take me through your logic again.'

'Craig, I haven't got time for this.'

'Come on, Scott. What makes you think Turnbull Senior is at risk?'

'Jen Black killed his son. Clonked him on the head then suffocated him. She watched him die. That's cold, hard revenge.'

'So, what do we do now?'

Cullen checked for traffic then jogged across the road. A row of cottages with big front gardens, out of place on a teeming high street. Certainly no signs of life in the flat above the butcher's. He crossed back over.

'Doesn't look like he's inside.' Hunter looked round at Cullen. 'You want to break in?'

'I'll get annihilated if we do.'

'You don't think she's got him in there?'

'Sod it.' Cullen got out his phone and called Tommy Smith.

It just rang and rang. Christ, he'd gone home for the evening. Cullen sifted through his emails and found the invite to Tommy's impending retirement bash. Bingo — mobile number for RSVPing.

'What the hell do you want?' Sounded like he was in a bathroom.

'Charming.' Cullen tried to keep his voice level. 'Tommy, I need a trace on that mobile number for Jenny Black.'

'Told you, she's in Spain.'

'Really?'

'Well, her phone is.'

Cullen stared at the butcher's again, trying to tell himself that this wasn't just another policeman's hunch. No — even if Richard Turnbull wasn't in there, he was still under threat. 'Can you run a check on another number for me? Richard Turnbull?'

'That the Richard Turnbull that wee Elvis was asking about?'

'Possibly.' Cullen had no idea what Elvis was up to. Probably crap for Bain.

'Give me a sec, then.' Sounded like water splashing.

'Are you on the toilet?'

'I'm in the bath. Got it set up so I can play *Football Manager* on my laptop, resting on a stand.' He sighed. 'Or so I can deal with your last-minute nonsense. Okay, I've got Turnbull's mobile on just now and it's hitting two cell sites in Gilmerton. I'd say it's the high street there.'

Cullen swung around, desperately searching for nearby phone masts. 'There's a high street here?'

'Alright, what passes for one. Gilmerton Road. You see the Domino's Pizza?'

'Right.' And Cullen could see the other mobile mast in the park over the road. Meaning the phone was there. 'Perfect.'

'What's this about, Scott?'

'Just make sure that trace goes in my inbox tonight.'

'You still haven't sent me that RIPSA you're due me.'

'I'll do it tonight with another one.'

'Such a chancer.'

'Good luck keeping Hearts up, Tommy.'

'Swirling round the plughole, mate. Bye.' And he was gone.

Cullen tried to process it all. Turnbull was here. No way of knowing if Jenny Black was. Assuming she was behind this. 'Think we should go in?'

'What's the worst that can happen?'

'Me working for Bain again.' Cullen tried a smile, but it felt forced. 'The worst that happens is we break in on a man asleep. Or on the toilet.'

'Or having sex.'

'Done all three before. Once with two of the three.'

'Shagging on the bog?'

'No, sleeping.' Cullen didn't see any other options here. 'Okay, let's do this.'

'Just like old times.'

'I'm not your Acting DC, Craig, so you're busting that door down. I still have a sore shoulder from that gym case.'

'That was a long time ago, mate. You should strengthen up.' Hunter grabbed the handle and twisted. The door opened. 'Well, that'll save wear and tear on your old man's body.'

Cullen gestured for him to go first.

Like stepping into a freezer. It had that meaty sawdusty smell, mixed with industrial cleaners. The meat was all covered up for the night under plastic sheeting. Two doors at the back, one marked "Bathroom", the other one led to the flat Cullen and Angela had been to that morning. He opened the door and held it. The stairs led up, but there was another room, marked "Store".

Hunter stopped dead. 'You hear that?'

All Cullen could pick up was the hum of the fridges and the blue fly zapper on the wall. 'Hear what?'

'People talking.'

Cullen heard someone say, 'eat it'.

'Come on.' Hunter snapped out his baton. Always looked so much cooler than when Cullen did it. Then again, he'd actually killed people so maybe it wasn't so cool.

Cullen followed suit, but his baton cracked loud.

A sharp 'shhhh' came from inside the back room.

Hunter pushed against the wall at the other side of the door.

Cullen took the handle and yanked, then eased the door open.

Inside, a woman was sitting on a chair, reaching around Richard Turnbull, propped up, his back resting against her knees. She was stuffing glistening meat into his mouth, smearing it around his lips. 'Eat it!'

'Stop!' Cullen rushed forward, branding his baton like a club.

She dropped the packet of meat onto the floor and a blade flashed in her other hand. A butcher's knife, pressed against Turnbull's throat.

'Jenny Black?'

She nodded.

Cullen held up his hands, but didn't drop the baton. 'Just play this cool, okay? Nobody has to die here.'

Her eyes darted around the room. She was trapped and she knew it. Cullen followed her gaze, needing to know if there was anything that might spook her. No sign of Hunter. Good.

'Let him go then we can have a nice chat instead. Okay?'

She grabbed Turnbull's hair with her free hand and pulled his head back. God knows what she'd done to him, but he was out of it. Blood poured down his face, covering his eyes. 'You know what he did to me?'

'Let's talk about it elsewhere, Jenny. Okay?'

'He killed my daughter!'

'Jenny, it's okay. Just let him go and this will all be fine.'

'How can it be fine? He poisoned the meat I fed to Kayleigh. She died because of *him*.'

'If he did it, we'll—'

'HE DID IT!'

'Okay, but let's do this sensibly.'

Her free hand lashed out and something slopped against Cullen's cheek, then slid down and splatted off the floor. Looked like raw pork.

'You feed similar stuff to his son?'

'I wanted this animal to see what it was like to lose a child. I wish he could've seen the lights go out behind his eyes, like I did with Kayleigh.'

'Put the knife down and it'll all be—'

'No!' She pulled the knife back and drove the blade towards Turnbull's throat.

Another flash of steel and a loud clatter.

Then sixteen stone of monster flew past Cullen. Hunter took her down, grabbing her throat and driving her hard against the wall.

Cullen rushed into action. He grabbed Turnbull and pulled him up onto the seat, then opened his lips wide and clawed at the meat. It was lodged into his throat. God knows if he'd swallowed any. Cullen clawed at it, pulling the meat out.

But Turnbull wasn't breathing.

He reached into his pocket for his phone and hit dial.

23

BAIN

Simon Mowat won't even look at us. Prize chump, this boy. He's tracing a knot on the tabletop with his finger-nails. One's really long, like he bumps coke with it. 'I need to see my mother.' Got to take pity on the boy.

I look over at Elvis but he's perplexed. Only way to describe it. 'She's in great care.' I hold the boy's gaze, but those are dead eyes. 'DC Caldwell is one of my finest officers.'

'I don't care. It needs to be me there. I need to make sure she takes her meds.'

Sounds like the boy's missed a dose of his own. I chuck the CCTV still on the table. 'Son, we know what you were up to at the shop. Some really shady business.'

'I bought six cans of energy drink.' Christ and it looks like he's tanned the lot of them. Is that what I look like when I do the same? Fuck. 'That's not a crime!'

'No, you tried to mis-price a steak. It's fraud.'

'You've got no proof.'

'It's all on CCTV.' I tap the victim on the page. Time was, I'd have been in the PM to see Deeley cut him up, but now it's fuckin' Sundance's job, isn't it? 'This boy was murdered.'

'Oh.'

'That's it?'

'I didn't do it!'

'What did you do?'

'Nothing. I was buying a steak for my mother. She needs lots of iron and protein because of her condition. Usually I give her poached eggs, but she's getting fed up of them.'

'You speak to this boy?'

'Just to ask when they're reducing stuff.'

'So you can thieve another sirloin?'

'No!'

I lean over to the mic and check my watch. 'Interview paused at eighteen oh seven.' I stay standing. 'We're away for a cup of coffee. You might want to think about talking here because, as I see it, you're up to your oxters in this.'

But he's back to tracing his imaginary faces on the desk.

'Come on.' I open the door for Elvis, then follow him out. 'For fuckin' crying out loud.'

'You can't think he's killed the lad over some reduced steak?'

'I've seen dafter things.'

I'm fucked here. Thought this was our boy, but he's just a poor sap with a sick mother. Join the fuckin' club. Sundance and Crystal will be all over us for this. My moby has missed calls from the pair of them. Shite almighty indeed.

'Right, let's go back to first principles.' I stare at the CCTV still of that Simon Mowat boy arguing with Philip Turnbull, our victim.

'Bri, no matter how desperate you are to prove that he's our killer, if he isn't, he just isn't.'

Elvis has a point but I'm not giving him the satisfaction.

So I stare at the image again. The boy's standing there, and it's like he clocks Turnbull approaching, which is what makes him fuck off in a few frames time. Got a basket with some tins of drink in them, fine, but... 'What's he holding in his other hand?'

Elvis takes the sheet and squints at it. 'No idea.' And he's off, charging down the corridor, then into the meeting room he's block booked all day.

Have to fuckin' jog to catch him. 'What's up?'

But Elvis is in the fuckin' zone, doing that weird focus thing. Legs kinked around the legs of the chair, fingers battering the keyboard. Then he looks up at us with wide eyes. 'Check this out.'

I can't see fuck all, just the light shining off his screen. I crouch down and, aha, he's playing the CCTV of the supermarket. Pretty much paused on the frame we'd printed, maybe a few seconds later.

'Bri, it looks like a bag.'

'A bag?'

'A tote bag.' He zooms in and blows up a pixelly mess. 'Says Bloody Scotland 2019.'

'What the fuck is that?'

'A crime writing festival.'

'I see. And why's that good for us?'

'Don't know.' The idiot's blushing, but he's back in the zone, working that laptop like my old man in the factory he worked in for his whole puff. 'Right, what the fuck is that?' He leans back and lets us at the screen again.

The boy, Simon fuckin' Mowat, is up to some shady shite, that's for sure.

24

CULLEN

Alistair Reynolds still looked like he needed a babysitter—all smooth skin, baby-blue eyes and perfectly weighted dark hair—and yet he was defending Jenny Black. Not that he was actively doing much, just sitting there and scribbling on a notepad with a cracked biro. 'Is Mr Turnbull going to live?' He didn't look up.

'We don't know yet.' Cullen shrugged. 'He's at the hospital just now.'

Jenny Black sat there, arms folded. She wore a T-shirt like she was actually going to Spain, and not staying in grim, dark Gilmerton. Hard to believe she was Adam Searle's wife and not his daughter, but her record showed she was actually older than him. 'I see.'

'That's it? That's all you're going to give us?'

'You found me. You must know what that vermin did to me and my family.'

'Your husband told us quite a lot of things.' Cullen narrowed his eyes at her. 'You might want to thank him, though, as he's done a fantastic job of covering for you. Despite speaking to us on several occasions, he didn't think to tell us about your daughter.'

That just bounced off her. She'd internalised the trauma so much that the mention of it didn't affect her. It just motivated her to murder.

'If you've got it all from Adam, why are you even talking to me?'

'You've got a right to a fair trial.'

'Doesn't feel very fair if he can just kill my daughter and get away with it.'

'How about you share the proof with us?'

'What proof?'

'That he was responsible for the poisoning that killed your daughter.'

She looked away, eyes narrowing.

'If you've got evidence that Mr Turnbull was behind the poisoning, then now's the time to share it.'

She pounded her fists off the table. The din echoed round the room, but nobody said anything. She rubbed at her wrists, bruised from where Hunter's baton had disarmed her.

'I want to listen to your side of this, Ms Black. Please.'

She shook her head. 'After we lost Kayleigh, I was a complete mess. Everything was black. It was all ruined. And then… I got therapy. Started to see the light. But I just couldn't speak to Adam and we were so far apart, and it was so raw being in that flat. So I moved out of our old home. And I started to pull everything together. Went back to work.'

'Was that when you met Philip Turnbull?'

'Right.' She leaned back, eyes shut. 'I blame him.'

'You think Philip was involved?'

'I never had any proof, but of course I knew. It was obvious, wasn't it? Phil was put up to it by his father. His business was collapsing due to the aggressive price war going on. Ashworth's were trying to force local businesses to close. Happens a lot.'

'Turned around since then.'

'Exactly. Richard Turnbull was getting his son to poison the meat when he was alone in the store to put out the bread in the morning.'

'Your husband tell you this?'

'Might as well have.'

'Did Phil?'

'I don't know what you mean.'

'We know that you two were an item.'

'Right.' She sighed. 'This is before I realised. One day, *he* came in to the office at work, trying to change his director of studies. I recognised him from the store, got chatting to him. Went for a drink, and one thing led to another.'

'You went to his place.'

'A couple of times. Flat on World's End Close. Didn't want to take him to mine because, well. The neighbours. I was on the rebound from what happened with Adam, but I ruined my career. That little shit stole my key, broke into the office and photocopied the exam paper. And he was stupid enough to get caught.'

Cullen realised it all came down to keys. 'And you stole the cleaner's key?'

'Not exactly difficult. He was so baked, I just walked in there while he watched some stupid video on YouTube. Thought I was a ghost.'

'How did you get hold of my locker key?'

'I've no idea what you're talking about.'

'Sure?'

'Sure.'

'You've not got a friendly cop in here?'

'No. Listen, I killed Philip because his father is responsible for my daughter's death. I killed his son and now he's going to die. Good riddance.'

'Mr Turnbull is going to pull through.'

She deflated. All the fire in her eyes snuffed out in an instant.

25

BAIN

W hat in the name of side-saddle fucknuttery has happened here?

Sundance and Crystal are standing by the window, chatting under their breaths about something or other. Behind them, a nurse is checking out Turnbull senior's drip. Crystal looks fucking raging though. At quite what, I couldn't possibly even begin to wonder.

Cough, bollocks.

Shite, did that out loud. Pair of them are now looking at us.

Sundance slips inside the room, but Crystal comes over to us. 'Brian, what are you doing here?'

I lean against the wall and fold my arms, trying to act all casual. 'Catching up with you pair.'

Methven stares hard right at us. Snide prick. 'I've been calling you.'

I get out my mobile. 'Beauty of these bad boys is they tell who who's been calling you.'

'And yet you didn't return the call?'

'Been busy.'

'Do you know anything about the meat?'

'The meat that Anderson lost?'

'That. It turned up in DI Cullen's locker.'

'Well, it wasn't me! Why would I take it?'

'You have a well-documented axe to grind with DI Cullen.'

'Used to, maybe. I'm a changed man, Col. Can see he's going to be a good DI. Harsh that you're roasting him for losing the meat in the first place, mind.'

'We were lucky to obtain a confession from the perpetrator.' Crystal points through the glass to where Richard Turnbull is being tended to. 'And we were incredibly lucky he didn't lose his life.'

'Nah, Col. That's not lucky, that's good policing. Solid work.'

He looks at us like I'm up to something. Maybe I am, but I'm the fuckin' master here. He's just a useless fanny who thinks he's the Boy.

Sundance comes back out. 'They think they've got all the meat out of his guts.'

'What was it?'

'Pork.'

'Not the meat, the fuckin' poison!'

'Oh, strychnine.'

'How the fuck does someone get hold of that?'

Crystal's doing that fuckin' annoying thing where he shuts his eyes and makes the lids flutter. 'In this day and age, you can get anything you want from anywhere, anytime you want.'

'Aye, well. Always the lassies, isn't it?'

'Excuse me?'

'Poisoning. Boys will smash someone's head in, run them

over in a car, shoot them, that kind of thing. Lassies, it's always the poisoning.'

They look at each other like there's been a chat. Kind of expected there has been. Snidey wankers.

As much as I want to leave them in suspense, I can't help myself. 'Trouble is, the way I hear it, your lassie thinks those two were the ones poisoning the meat in the shop, right?'

Crystal's raging, looking at us like I've mis-filed a report or something. 'What have you got, Brian?'

'Just wanted to congratulate you on solving a murder. Good work, Sundance. I must've taught you well.'

He's taking it like a dose of fuckin' salts. Smiling, but he's fucking raging inside. 'Thank you.'

'I mean, I solved three murders.'

Prick looks at Crystal then back at me. 'What?'

'Just the small matter of getting a full confession for the meat poisoning.' With a regal flourish, I hand over the photo of the boy in the supermarket. 'That lad there. Simon Mowat. We spotted him on CCTV swapping out meat from a carrier. Spoke to him and he crumpled.'

Another look between them, but it's like they're out of control. This isn't what the pair of fannies expected.

'Boy confessed right away, never mind crumpled. He's an inadequate personality, and the only time he felt higher than an amoeba was when he killed. Trouble is, once it's all done and dusted, he just goes back to being wee Simon Mowat. When we mentioned swapping in meat, he switched back to the poisoner and went into great detail about his methods so he could take all the perceived credit. But he's a full-time carer for his sick mother, gets paid for it but not much. He told me and Elvis that poisoning was the only time he feels in control. For a day, he can feel like a god. He killed three people back then, but stopped it. This is him starting up again.'

They're floored by this. Much as I'd love to bask in it for a long time, I'd better get on with the show.

'The boy found his dad's warchest of old-time rat poison going to waste in the garden shed. Dad died about ten years back and his mother went into a slow decline. Sneaky bugger is slowly feeding the stuff to her as well, trying to get his nerve up to top the old dear. Much easier to do a load of randoms in a supermarket than her. Must be sentimental, I guess.'

Sundance clears his throat. 'Well, that's excellent work, Brian.'

'Don't mention it, Scott.' I wrap my arms around him to hug him, but mainly so I can slip the spanner's locker key back in his suit pocket.

EPILOGUE

CULLEN

'Why do I want to become a detective again?' Sergeant Lauren Reid stared up at the ceiling with a coy look on her face. She was perched on the edge of the desk with perfect posture, hands resting on the surface, bright orange nails and a giant diamond on her ring finger. She wore standard uniform, T-shirt with a fleece, though she had draped two coats on the back of the seat. 'Okay.' She focused on Cullen and sat back, her dark-blonde ponytail flopping over her left shoulder. 'Well, I was a detective constable in Thames Valley for eighteen months before my now-husband got a job in Edinburgh. We decided it was best for me to move up, and a uniform sergeant position became available.'

Donna Nichols sat to Cullen's right, scribbling away in the interview pack. Hair in a bun, eyes lined, wearing a trouser suit that struggled with her bulging, pregnant belly. 'Go on?'

Lauren frowned at Cullen. 'Well, I, um, I was good at being

a detective. I enjoyed it. Part of this uniform role is it's allowed me to manage a team and, while it's not developed my detective skills, it has let me broaden my skillset as a leader.'

Cullen glanced at Donna and got a nod, so he smiled at Lauren. 'Okay, that's all of our questions. Have you got any for us?'

Lauren sat forward and rubbed her arms like she was in the deep freeze back at the supermarket. 'I was just wondering if you had a timescale on this?'

'Well.' Donna slammed her notes shut like a door. 'We're interviewing a few other candidates. Have you got other irons in the fire, as it were?'

'Possibly.'

'Okay, well, this kind of thing can take weeks if not months, especially if the worst comes to the worst with the global situation. It's late February, who knows where we'll be in a month's time.'

'Okay.' She held Cullen's gaze for a few seconds, her eyes twitching like she was conveying some message. 'Well, that's all for me.'

The door opened and Methven stood there, his wild eyebrows like they were receiving a signal from deep space. 'A word.' He slipped off and the door shut.

Cullen walked over but stopped by the door. 'Thanks for coming in, Sergeant. I'll see you around.'

'Thanks.'

Cullen left them to it, but there was no sign of Methven. The blinds shuffled in the meeting room next door and Cullen clocked those eyebrows, so he followed him in. 'That interview went well.'

'Good.' But Methven didn't seem too keen to hear it. He was over by the window, staring out, his jaw clenched tight.

'You know I didn't take that meat, right?'

'I know. Mr Anderson is getting hauled over the coals for it.

He's been obsessing about productivity gains and what have you, but his office didn't even have a security camera. That place should've been locked down, but... it wasn't.' Still staring out, Methven shook his head. 'But we've got a good idea who did take it.'

Cullen joined Methven by the window. Bain was standing by his purple Mondeo, laughing and joking with Elvis. 'And there he is.'

Methven swivelled round to look at Cullen. 'So we are on the same page.'

Of course it was Bain. Cullen knew it from the start, deep in his soul, but he had no evidence. Did Methven? 'Can we get rid of him?'

'That's the thing.' Methven pulled the roller blind down to block their view of Bain. 'As you know, I've spent all afternoon in calls pertaining to a case in Dundee and Carolyn... Well, she called me personally to thank me for my assistance in the matter.' A dark look passed across his face like a cloud. 'She also imparted some information, namely that DS Bain is to remain in his post.'

Cullen laughed. 'Are you serious?'

'Extremely. Do you think I'm one to joke? Carolyn has his back.'

'Great.' Cullen couldn't face up to another day with Bain, let alone another year or two. 'What, you think he's got something on her?'

'I hate to think what.'

'So Bain is blackmailing the head of Specialised Crime?'

'I wouldn't put anything past him.' Methven left the window and took the seat at the head of the table, facing Cullen. 'I did some digging. They served together in Glasgow for a few years.'

'We knew that, didn't we? It's why he was kept on in Glasgow after you got his old job.'

'Well, either way, it probably means he knows something he

shouldn't, or something she did that might cause issues for her. Rumour is she's going for one of the assistant chief constable positions.'

'You any idea what her dirty laundry is?'

'No, but for her it's best burned in the back garden.' Methven took out his phone and inspected a message, then put it away.

'What do I do about Lauren?'

'Well, I'll sort that out.'

'She's a good cop. I'd like her on my team.'

'And I shall sort that out, Scott. Carolyn alluded to some increase in my headcount, so I shall see if that will permit us to take her on while we manage the situation with DS Bain.'

'So we're stuck with him?'

'Not quite. While DS Bain getting to the bottom of this poisoning scandal makes things a lot more difficult for us, I have no doubt that he was behind the missing meat farrago. He's gunning for you, Scott. You've got his old position, ergo he wants it back.'

The logic was sound. 'And you had his old position?'

'Correct.'

'So you want to snare him in something?'

'That's the plan, yes.'

'You got any ideas?'

Methven grinned wide. 'Oh yes.'

ACKNOWLEDGMENTS

Without the following, this book wouldn't exist:

Development Editing
Allan Guthrie

Procedural Analysis
James Mackay

Copy Editing
Allan Guthrie, Kitty Harrison

Proofing
John Rickards

As ever, infinite thanks to Kitty for putting up with me and all of my nonsense.

CULLEN & BAIN WILL RETURN IN

"HELL'S KITCHEN"

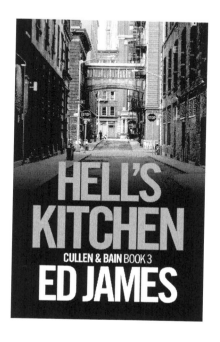

August 1st 2020

If you enjoyed this book, please consider leaving a review on Amazon.

If you would like to be kept up to date with new releases from Ed James, please fill out a contact form.

SEE ANOTHER SIDE OF SCOTT CULLEN IN

"MISSING"

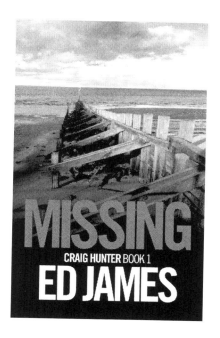

Out now!

Cullen features heavily in MISSING, a police procedural comedy thriller starring Craig Hunter, ex-soldier and ex-CID, now back in uniform.

It's out now and you can get a copy at Amazon.